EASTER STORIES FOR KIDS

12 Exciting Easter Tales
for Adventurous Kids

NATHAN SNYDER

CONTENTS

INTRODUCTION

When you think of Easter, what do you think of first?

The chances are that one of the first things you'll imagine will be chocolate - or rather, chocolate eggs, in particular.

Or maybe you think of Easter egg hunts? What about straw baskets full to the brim with candies and other sweet treats?

Or maybe you think of the Easter Bunny himself, bounding from town to town, leaving Easter eggs for all of us to find on Easter morning.

Or perhaps you imagine springtime itself when you think of Easter, and end up picturing fields full of spring flowers, trees full of blossom, and fields full of young rabbits, lambs, chicks, and calves?

Any one of these would be a perfectly good answer, of course - which is just as well, as every one of them features in the twelve Easter stories that follow!

From an Easter egg hunt that goes terribly wrong to an Easter surprise - and from some rabbits who decide to take a trip to see if the Easter Bunny is real or not, to some animals who decide to take Easter into their own hands (or rather, claws…) - the tales here cover everything you could possibly imagine when you think of Easter morning!

So, let's begin, once upon a time, with our very first Easter tale….

THE RABBIT IN THE HAT

The Great Splendido was one of the world's most talented magicians. For years he had astounded audiences in every corner of the globe with his extraordinary tricks, mind-boggling illusions, and flabbergasting feats of magical prowess.

In that time, his tricks had only become bigger, bolder, and even more remarkable. While other magicians were amazing audiences by simply linking sets of metal hoops together, the Great Splendido had begun performing his version of the same trick with enormous red-hot iron rings, which he would pull out of a blazing fire while on stage without ever being burned. While all other illusionists were still busy sawing a lady in half while she was encased in a wooden box - with her head smiling at one end, and her feet still happily wriggling away at the other - the Great Splendido had started repeating the same trick with a roaring, growling, and not-quite-so-happy grizzly bear. And when other magicians had started copying the Great Splendido's signature card trick - pulling the ace of spaces out of a pack of cards, shuffled by someone from the audience, while he was blindfolded - he had upped his game once more, and begun performing a new version of his classic ace-of-spades trick while riding a unicycle and juggling half a dozen burning wooden clubs in the air. Even the climax of his show - a recreation of the first trick he had ever learned, pulling a giant white rabbit out of his top hat - was now bigger and better than ever before. Now, as well as magically producing a rabbit out of nowhere, the Great Splendido would end his act with doves flying out of his jacket sleeves, and sparks and fireworks shooting from hidden pockets in his shoulders. Truly, his was an amazing show to behold.

Not that he could do all of that on his own, of course. While he was busy onstage wrestling bears into boxes and setting fire to his jugglers' clubs, all the time, sat backstage, was his faithful assistant, Gerald.

It was Gerald's job, always out of sight of the audience, to prepare everything the Great Splendido would need for his next trick - setting up the equipment, and cueing the music - so that his grand magic show went off without a hitch. Gerald knew all the Great Splendido's secrets. For more than 40 years he had rehearsed and rehearsed and rehearsed with the Great Splendido, over and over again, until they were both so well practiced that his show always went as smoothly and as effortlessly as possible. All their hard work had paid off, too, as the Great Splendido was now not only one of the world's finest magicians, but one of its most successful too. He was constantly in high demand, and invitations were constantly arriving at his home, asking him to come and perform his extraordinary magic show in towns and cities and countries all over the world.

In fact, it was one of these invitations that arrived in the Great Splendido's mailbox (along with a bill for bear food and an advertisement for foldable paper flowers and strings of colored flags) early one spring morning. As he sat flicking through his post while he ate his breakfast, the invitation immediately caught his eye.

It was in a thick, cream-colored envelope, on which his address was written in glistening golden ink. The envelope had been sealed with a large wax seal too, on which was stamped what appeared to be some kind of coat of arms. The Great Splendido threw down his toast and excitedly tore open the envelope. It was remarkable news. Inside was an invitation to perform his magic show in front of the king and queen themselves, at their palace, as part of their Easter weekend celebrations the following month.

The Great Splendido could hardly contain his excitement. Forgetting all about his breakfast, he ran over to the telephone and eagerly began dialing the number of his ever-faithful assistant, Gerald. "The King and Queen!", he muttered to himself, as the phone rang. "In the palace! And on Easter weekend!" *Ring, ring. Ring, ring.* "We shall have to rehearse! Every day!" The Great Splendido determined. *Ring, ring. Ring, ring.* "We simply cannot afford a single mistake in such a wonderful venue!"

And *still,* the phoneline rang. And rang. And rang.

"That's odd," the Great Splendido said. "It's so early in the morning, Gerald should still be at home, surely. Where on earth could he be?"

Unfortunately, he would soon find out. The Great Splendido hung up the phone, but almost it immediately began ringing. "Gerald!" He exclaimed as he answered it. "Where were you, my friend, I was beginning to worry! We have work to do! Work, I say! We must rehearse and rehearse and rehearse until so we have the greatest show imaginable! What do I always say, Gerald? The rehearsal is everything. Everything! Now, when are you free?"

There was silence on the other end of the phone.

"Gerald?" The Great Splendido said, "Hello, are you there?"

"Oh," came a woman's voice. It was thin and quiet, not at all like the voice the Great Splendido was expecting. "Mr. Splendido, I'm so sorry," the voice said. "This is Alice. I'm afraid—I'm afraid Gerald isn't well. He's had an accident."

"Alice!" the Great Splendido exclaimed, suddenly recognizing the voice of his assistant's wife at the other end of the line. "An accident?! Good gracious, what manner of an accident?!"

"Yes, I..., I'm sorry," Alice continued, "he tripped on the stairs here at our home, and he fell and broke his ankle. He'll be fine, I'm sure, but I'm afraid he's in hospital and will be for quite some time, the doctors say. They have his leg in traction - it's all bandaged up, hanging from the ceiling in some bizarre contraption, it really is the strangest thing to see...."

"Oh, my word!" The Great Splendido responded, "that is dreadful news! Simply dreadful! Alice, I must go and see him immediately. My poor Gerald! A broken ankle, indeed. Oh, these things really do happen when you least expect them to, do they not? And when you can least *afford* them to happen too, I should say, because Alice - I have had the most extraordinary invitation only just this morning, and Gerald and I simply must have my show in absolutely tip-top standard by this time next month! A mere matter of weeks away! Weeks, I say! I'm going to need all his help, Alice, more than ever before really, to ...."

"Oh, a–about that," interrupted Alice. "Yes, yes..., about that. I..., well, *we*, really, *we*. We've been meaning to tell you for quite some time now," she continued, "but we both think it's about time Gerald thought about retiring...."

The Great Splendido paused, his mouth hanging open. "Retiring!" He exclaimed, "Gerald...! Now...?"

"...and this accident," Alice went on. "It's only made us think even more that now really is the time for Gerald to be putting his feet up - er, so to speak, not like he has at the moment, you understand...."

"Oh, my dear, but Gerald simply cannot retire! He is the ace to my jack! The star to my moon! We've worked together so long, I simply cannot imagine - I mean, we have this royal performance next month, and where I go, he goes, you understand, and..., and...." The Great Splendido paused again. The years of faithful assistance Gerald had provided him ran through his mind, and he suddenly realized what he was saying, and the time at which he was saying it. "And..... And... Ah...." He sighed. "And, my dear Alice, you must do what is right for you both, of course, you must. I shall miss him greatly, of course, but I am taking up all his time. From you, indeed. I wish you both the longest and happiest of retirements."

"Oh, thank you," Alice said. The Great Splendido could hear the relief in her voice. "Thank you, very much. And I'm sure you shall find a new assistant, Mr. Splendido - one who is just as hard-working as my husband."

"I am sure I shall, Alice," he replied. "Thank you." He hung up the phone and glanced around him at the posters and playbills and newspaper clippings that covered the walls of his home. "Well, now," he said to himself. "A new assistant, it is."

****

Finding a replacement for Gerald proved somewhat harder than the Great Splendido had anticipated, however. With just a matter of weeks, until he was due to perform at the palace, he immediately sprang into action and began calling upon every contact in his address book, rang around every theatre in which he had every performed, and placed an advertisement in every newspaper he could think of. Hundreds of letters and phone calls followed, and in the days that followed the Great Splendido was inundated with countless applications from every corner of the world, all from people wanting to be his next assistant. But as he narrowed his search down to a shortlist, and began meeting and auditioning with all the very best people who had applied, it soon became clear that Gerald was to prove an all but impossible act to follow.

One man, for instance, had managed to trap himself in the Great Splendido's magic box during his audition, leaving the bear roaming the stage with a saw in its mouth in his place. Another had somehow managed to set the stage curtain on fire while preparing the Great Splendido's flaming rings illusion. And yet another had tried to copy the Great Splendido's blindfold unicycle trick by unicycling blindfolded himself - only to crash through the stage door and disappear off down the street, with playing cards flying out of his pockets. It took the Great Splendido over an hour to find him, lying in a crumpled heap in a ditch with the wheel of the unicycle stuck around his head. The auditioning process had, quite simply, proved a disaster.

As the weeks shortened into days and the King and Queen's Easter show crept ever closer, the Great Splendido found himself feeling increasingly uneasy about what lay ahead. Having turned down everyone who had applied to be his new assistant, he found himself facing the very real prospect of mounting his magic show all on his own.

One evening, he sat at home in his study, surrounded by textbooks of magic tricks and blueprints of his tricks and contraptions, mulling over his predicament. "I guess I could handle the bear into the sawing box myself," he thought. "But then again - while I'm sawing him in half, who will be preparing the fire for my flaming rings illusion? They need to be glowing hot by the time I wheel them out on stage, after all, or else the trick doesn't work."

He looked down at the pile of failed applications on the table beside him, all of which had the word REJECTED stamped across them in bright red letters. "And while I'm linking the flaming rings," he went on, "someone needs to be backstage preparing my unicycle. And then the rabbit and the birds for my finale. Bah!" he exclaimed, snapping his fingers in frustration. "It is simply impossible. I must, *must* find myself a new assistant!" He looked down once more at the disastrous line of applicants he had already dismissed and sighed.

Just at that moment, the doorbell rang. The Great Splendido furrowed his brow and looked up at the clock on his wall. "Odd," he muttered to himself, as he made his way to his door. "I wasn't expecting any guests this evening?"

Outside, stood on his doorstep, was a young man of perhaps no more than 18 or 19 years. He was dressed in a somewhat old-fashioned and ill-fitting suit, and his black hair was slicked down in a severe side-parting. In his hand, held what looked to be a cutting from a newspaper. "Mr. Splendido?" The man asked nervously.

"Yes?" The Great Splendido answered, looking his curious visitor up and down.

"My name is Charles. Charles Bugg. I'm here - well, I'm here because I saw your advertisement in the newspaper, and I've always wanted to try my hand at magic, you see, and I thought…."

"Oh, the assistant's job?" The Great Splendido interrupted. "You've come to apply to be my new assistant?"

"Yes, sir, Mr. Splendido!" Charles replied enthusiastically. "You see, I've always wanted to be a magician, ever since I first saw perform your show when I was a boy. And ever since then, I've spent every day designing and making my magic tricks, just like you did when you were my age. Like this one!" At that moment, Charles reached inside his jacket and pulled out a somewhat sorry-looking bunch of spring-loaded paper flowers, that burst out of their hiding place inside his lapel in a lackluster shower of confetti and torn petals. The Great Splendido looked on unimpressed.

"And - and then of course, there's this," Charles went on, undaunted, as he reached into his other jacket pocket and pulled out a pack of cards. He began fumblingly shuffling and riffling them between his hands. "Think of a card, any card," he said. "But don't tell me - I'll be able to deduce what it is using magic!" He explained excitedly, as he tried finally to spray the cards from one hand to the other, but succeeded only in launching the entire pack in one long stream into the Great Splendido's face. "Oh, no, I'm so sorry!" he muttered, as the cards tumbled to the ground. "Was…er, was that your card?" Charles said hopefully, pointing to the two of hearts that had become lodged in the Great Splendido's shirt collar.

The Great Splendido closed his eyes and sighed as he removed the card. "No, I'm afraid it wasn't."

"Oh," Charles replied downheartedly. "That…, that trick usually goes a little better than that, I have to admit. I think I need to practice more, really. Because as you always say in your interviews, the rehearsal is everything!"

The Great Splendido paused for a moment. He had thought about politely declining Charles' application and quietly closing the door. But remembering his predicament - and seeing Charles' obvious enthusiasm, if his somewhat clumsy skill - he thought better of it. "Hmm," he said after a moment. "Fine. Let's try this out, shall we? Come on in, please. Would you like some tea?"

For the rest of the evening, he and Charles sat together, and talked for hour after hour about magic and magic tricks, with Charles showing off more of his somewhat awkward skills, and the Great Splendido offering him his advice and guidance. Despite his somewhat shambolic doorstep audition, Charles' enthusiasm soon proved infectious and the Great Splendido warmed to his unexpected guest. "Tell me," the Great Splendido asked, "if you were to become a magician like me, as you say you would like, what would be your aim? Your dream?"

Charles thought for a moment. "I believe I would like to come up with a trick that even you wouldn't know how to perform, Mr. Splendido. Something so remarkable that you would ask me to teach you it."

"Ha! What a marvelous answer," the Great Splendido laughed. "Charles, I like your enthusiasm. That settles it." He rose grandly from his chair. "You, my man, shall be my new assistant."

Charles could scarcely hide his excitement. "Oh, my! Mr. Splendido, thank you! Do you really mean it? I can't believe it!"

"But I should say," the Great Splendido warned, "before you get too excited, Charles, there is a lot for you to learn - and not a lot of time in which to learn it. We have work to do, Charles, a great deal of work. I shall need you here, bright and early tomorrow morning to make a start, and probably every day after that until Easter Day, do you hear? Because I have a very important performance lined up."

"Oh, no problem at all, Mr. Splendido," Charles beamed. "You can count on me!"

****

The following day, Charles remained true to his word and duly headed to the Great Splendido's home first thing in the morning. He arrived to find the door open, the hallway inside filled with dozens of dust-covered boxes and crates, containing all manner of magical equipment. The house was filled with a bizarre mixture of smells and sounds - sawing, roaring, cooing, and the noise of heavy things being hauled across the wooden floor. "Charles, is that you?" The Great

Splendido shouted from somewhere inside, "come in, my boy, come in. We have so much to do!"

Charles' first day was intense. He could scarcely have imagined how many things there were to learn, to practice, and to prepare in advance, and with the added pressure of the upcoming Easter performance, he soon found he had his work cut out for him.

He had to learn the secrets behind each and every trick. He had to learn the music that accompanied them all. He had to memorize the order in which the Great Splendido liked to perform them, and what needed preparing for the next trick, backstage, while the current trick was being performed onstage. He had to learn how to cage a bear, how to safely light a juggler's club, and how best to hide two dozen doves inside the lining of a jacket - and not forgetting a large white rabbit in a magician's top hat. And that was just for starters.

Despite the workload though, Charles quickly proved an excellent student, and within a matter of days, with his help and hard work, the Great Splendido's show was running almost as smoothly as ever.

At long last, the Easter weekend rolled around, and the day of the royal performance finally arrived. On the afternoon of

Easter Sunday, Charles and the Great Splendido made their way to the palace - along with a whole truckload of magical paraphernalia - and there, behind a curtain in one of the royal ballrooms that had been filled with chairs for the assembling audience, they began to prepare for the performance. Backstage, Charles could hear the chattering of the audience grow as more and more guests arrived and took their seats. Before long, it was time for the curtain to go up, and the sound of applause filled the room as the King rose to his feet and introduced the show.

"My invited guests," the King's voice rang out around the room, "what a pleasure we are all in for this Easter day. For performing for us all tonight is the greatest magician in my kingdom - if not, indeed, the world. The Great Splendido!"

At that sound, the curtain rose, the entrance music played, and the show began. As the Great Splendido strode out onto the stage - trailing a multicolored string of flags and streamers behind him - even he could feel the butterflies in his stomach as he looked down and saw the royal family eagerly applauding him.

He need not have been nervous, however, as all Charles' hard work paid off and the show went off without a hitch. He had stoked the fire perfectly well for the glowing rings illusion, and the audience had been duly astounded as the Great Splendido effortlessly connected them together on stage. The bear had been well-behaved as it had crawled into its box and the Great Splendido sawed it in half. And when the time came for his unicycling card trick, the crowd gasped as the Great Splendido cycled his way down off the front of the stage, and had the Queen herself select a card from the deck.

Eventually, there was just one trick left to perform: the Great Splendido's classic finale, pulling the rabbit out of his hat. Backstage, Charles was busy readying everything the Great Splendido would need - but there was a problem. Amid the chaos of moving all the props, manhandling a bear back into its enclosure, and stoking a burning firepit, the Great Splendido's white rabbit had somehow escaped its cage and was nowhere to be seen.

Charles searched desperately through all the crates, behind the lights, under the costume rails, behind the curtains, and below the chairs, but there was no sign of it. And then Charles saw something that filled him with dread: there, over in the corner of the cramped space backstage, was a small open window leading out into the palace grounds. The Great Splendido had had Charles open it the moment they had arrived that afternoon, in an effort to let some fresh air into the stuffy makeshift dressing rooms behind the stage - but while the air had come in, it seems the rabbit had gone out.

On stage, Charles could hear the Great Splendido finishing his second last trick. There were now just minutes before he would need his hat and his rabbit to complete the show in a typically fine fashion. Charles had no time to lose. Grabbing a large cloth sack that he found draped over one of the chairs backstage, he ran over to the window, crouched down, and crawled outside.

It was cool and almost dark outside, with little more than the dim Easter moonlight illuminating the palace grounds. Charles narrowed his eyes and peered into the darkness, and began walking slowly over the grass, looking for anything even vaguely resembling a large white rabbit.

"Oh, no," Charles muttered to himself. "This is a disaster!" He glanced down at his watch. He reckoned he had maybe two minutes to get back inside and ensure everything was ready - but at that point, he saw it.

Some feet away from him, just beside an ornamental fountain in the middle of the palace gardens, sat a large white bunny rabbit. It seemed to be attracted to the running water of the fountain, and Charles watched as it stood up on its hind legs, and lent forward to take a drink from the shimmering pool beneath it.

"Got you!" Charles exclaimed as he bounded across the grass, leaping a small flowerbed and a wheelbarrow full of vegetables, and ran over to the fountain to bundle the Great Splendido's rabbit into the sack. "Good gracious!" he muttered to himself. "You're a lot heavier than I remember. When we get you back to the Great Splendido's house, you're going on a diet."

With the rabbit safely recaptured, Charles ran back towards the palace and crawled back through the tiny window into the Great Splendido's dressing room, just in time to see him exit the stage to ready himself for his grand finale.

"My hat!" The Great Splendido hissed. "Where is my hat? The music, cue the music. Where is my jacket?" With the music playing, Charles helped the Great Splendido into his long black tailcoat - the doves and fireworks already loaded into the sleeves and pockets - and, finally, emptied the sack into his top hat and plonked it (with the rabbit inside) down onto his head.

"My stars!" The Great Splendido exclaimed. "She wasn't as heavy as this yesterday!" He staggered a little as he adjusted the hat, trying not to make it too obvious that he had a gigantic rabbit weighing him down beneath it. "That's it - no more dandelion stalks for breakfast for her, this is ridiculous."

As the music swelled, the Great Splendido took a quick glance in the mirror, and - with Charles giving him a silent nod and two thumbs-up - he walked back out onto the stage for his finale.

"Ladies and gentlemen!" the Great Splendido began. "As you all know, it has long been a tradition for me to finish with one of the oldest of all magic tricks. My father taught me this trick long ago, and his father taught him it long before then. But just because a trick is old does not mean that it is any less special, or any less impressive. For you shall see…."

Charles watched nervously from behind a curtain at the side of the stage, as the Great Splendido raised his hat.

"First of all, this is nothing at all under my hat."

At this point, the Great Splendido removed his hat completely and tapped it with his wand as he showed how empty it was to the audience - all of whom immediately began to giggle.

Then chuckle. Then laugh. And then guffaw, riotously, until the entire ballroom was filled with the sound of their laughter.

"What? What's happening?" The Great Splendido muttered - before realizing that yes, his hat may well be empty, but the top of his head certainly wasn't.

The gigantic rabbit that Charles had found hopping around the palace gardens was now quite happily sitting on top of the Great Splendido's head, staring quizzically out at the assembled audience.

"Oh, good gracious!" The Great Splendido shouted. "Why, look at the size of this thing! This isn't my rabbit!" He began staggering around the stage, trying to shoo the rabbit from the top of his head - but the rabbit seemed entirely content just to sit there and take his curtain call.

"Shoo! Shoo, you giant old thing, shoo!"

As the Great Splendido waved his hands around, trying to rid himself of his giant attachment, the doves he had been saving for his finale suddenly began flying out of his sleeves and circling the audience. "Oh, the doves! Not now!" The Great Splendido cried out, "Charles, help - get this thing off my head!"

Charles ran out onto the stage to help, but as he reached the Great Splendido the fireworks hidden in his jacket suddenly ignited, and streams of glittering sparks began to shoot out of his shoulders and rain down onto the stage. "My finale!" The Great Splendido shouted out, as the noise of the audience's laughter grew even louder, and the music swelled to a crescendo.

In the chaos, the Great Splendido tripped on his coat tails and fell backwards, landing with a heavy thump on the floor of the stage, as doves continued to fly from his pockets and sparks continued to shoot out of his jacket. The rabbit seemed to be loving his time in the spotlight, and with the Great Splendido now sprawled on the floor, jumped down off his head and sat on his stomach looking out at the audience.

"Get this thing off me!" The Great Splendido called out. "My finale is ruined! Ruined!"

Charles ran across the stage, and lifted the gigantic rabbit from the Great Splendido's stomach - but as he did so, Charles felt something heavy drop from the rabbit's paws. A large, colorful egg landed on the floor of the stage with a thump, and then rolled slowly down towards the lights at the front of the stage, before rolling off the edge and onto the floor of the ballroom.

The Great Splendido sat up, staring at Charles holding the rabbit in his hands. "What was that?" he said.

Thump. Another egg landed on the stage, then slowly rolled down towards the audience. *Thump. Thump. Thump–thump.* More eggs began to fall from the rabbit, crashing down heavily onto the stage floor, before rolling off the front.

Charles looked as puzzled as the Great Splendido. The eggs seemed almost to be coming from somewhere within the rabbit's thick white fur - and there seemed to be an endless supply! Thump after thump after thump, more and more eggs began raining down from the rabbit and over the edge of the stage, until there was a large pile of them resting on the floor in front of the king and queen.

The audience was stupefied. The disastrous end to the Great Splendido's show, they seemed to presume, had all been fake - *this* was the real finale, they thought, and as they saw ever more colored easter eggs piling up and up and up in front of the stage, they could not believe their eyes. Their cheers and applause rang out louder than ever before.

"Amazing!" the King called out.

"Where are they all coming from?" The queen exclaimed in disbelief.

And still, they applauded. Seeing an opportunity to make the most of the disaster, the Great Splendido bounded to his feet and began to bow. "Ha, ha!" He laughed. "I had you all there, I bet!" He called out. "Charles - bow my friend! This is your applause too. And your friend the bunny rabbit has applause, of course!" Together, they bowed and bowed and bowed, until the audience's hands were sore from clapping, and the curtain fell on a truly memorable performance.

As soon as the show was over, Charles - still holding the rabbit in his hands - and the Great Splendido ran backstage. Charles placed the rabbit on top of a table, and it sat happily staring up at both of them.

"Oh, Splendido!" Charles said. "I'm so sorry! You see, your rabbit..., well, *this* rabbit. Oh, my apologies, only I..., I couldn't find it, and I saw the open window, and ...."

"Charles! Charles!" The Great Splendido exclaimed. "Why are you apologizing? Did you not hear the applause? This was an extraordinary finale! Those eggs! Where were they coming from? My stars, it was spectacular!"

"I..., I'm sorry?" Charles ventured, "I..., I thought I had..., or rather, I must have ruined the...."

"Ruined the show?! Goodness, no!" The Great Splendido laughed. "That was the best response to a finale I've ever heard! I only wish you'd explained this trick beforehand, so I might have been in on the joke! Now tell me, is this one of your own tricks? One of those you have designed yourself?"

"Trick?" Charles repeated. "My own trick?"

"Yes! Yes! You must tell me - just as you said when we first met, my boy," the Great Splendido went on. "You have to tell me. How on earth did you do it?"

THE HUNT FOR THE GOLDEN EGG

Easterburgh was a small town, far out in the middle of the countryside, miles away from any of the closest cities and villages.

Despite its isolation, the town -- which was so named because it was founded a great many years ago on an Easter Sunday - was home to quite a large number of people, who every Easter Sunday would come together and have a huge street party to celebrate both the Easter festival and the town's anniversary.

After years of celebrations, the 200th anniversary of Easterburgh's founding eventually rolled around. To make the occasion, the town council began planning an even more lavish celebration than ever before.

"This year's Easter party must be bigger than anything we have ever hosted!" The Lord Mayor decreed as he and his council members began brainstorming ideas for making the anniversary a day to remember. Finally, they hit upon what they thought was an excellent idea: a grand treasure hunt, with clues and maps scattered all over the town.

The day after the treasure hunt had been decided upon, the mayor headed out into the center of the town to announce his idea to the townspeople. "Ladies and gentlemen," he boomed from his lectern, standing in the middle of a stage in the marketplace. "I have the most splendid news! As you will all be aware, this year we shall be celebrating the two hundredth anniversary of the founding of our little town."

A cheer erupted from the people in the market square. "And," the mayor went on, calming the crowd with a wave of his hand, "we simply could not let such a momentous day go by without doing something extra special. So, as well as our usual Easter festival, I and my council will be organizing a special treasure hunt for you all, with clues hidden all over the town. The first person to find all the clues and work out where the treasure is hidden - hidden somewhere in Easterburgh - will win the grand prize: a golden Easter egg!"

The mayor reached inside the pocket of his gown and pulled out a glittering golden egg - perhaps two or three times the size of an ordinary chicken's egg - that shone and glistened brightly in the midday spring sunshine. The crowd gasped when they saw it. "Yes!" The mayor called out, "isn't it wonderful? And this time on Easter Day, one of you shall win it!"

"It'll be me!" Called out one man on the front row of the crowd, "I love a puzzle, I bet I'll solve it first."

"Don't be daft," cried out another voice, "I'll beat you any day of the week!"

"Well not with me playing too," called out someone else from further back.

"Yeah, and me too!" Someone else exclaimed. "The egg will be mine, mark my words!"

Before long, the entire crowd was shouting and jeering at one another, with everyone claiming that they would be the first to solve the clues and win the treasure.

"Oh, my," the mayor muttered to one of his attendants beside him. "I hope this is not going to get ugly. I didn't think the competition would be so fierce. It is only meant to be a little bit of fun, after all..."

The mayor again raised his hands to try to calm the crowd down. "Now, now, everyone...," he called out. "I'm sure you'll all do very well. But remember, this is all just a game. So let us just meet back here, all in the town square this Sunday morning, at 10 o'clock, and I'll give you the first clue then."

Over the days that followed, the treasure hunt for the golden egg understandably became the talk of the town. It was all anyone wanted to discuss. It was being talked about everywhere from the hair salon to the coffee shop, and from the blacksmiths to the fishmongers. And what's more, everyone was convinced that they and they alone would be able to outsmart everyone else and solve the clues better and faster than anyone.

Eventually, the Easter weekend came around and, to celebrate its anniversary, Easterburgh was decorated almost everywhere you could look, with flags, bunting, balloons, and streamers. The streets were lined with market stalls and kiosks, selling flowers, drinks, and all kinds of delicious food and sweet treats. But all that anyone wanted to talk about was the mayor's golden egg.

At 10 o'clock, the church bell rang out and the town all gathered in the market square as the mayor arrived to give out the first clue. "Good morning, everyone!" He boomed from the stage, "and a very happy anniversary to us all…," he called out.

"Get on with it!" A man in the crowd called back, as cheers and laughter filled the air.

The mayor gave a slightly disappointed smile. "Ah, yes, yes," he said, "alright let's get straight down to it and get this contest over with, shall we?"

He turned to another one of his attendants who stood beside him, who in turn, handed him a curled piece of thick while paper, tied up with a yellow ribbon. "Ah," the mayor said as he unfurled it. "Here we are then, clue number one," he cleared his throat and looked nervously out at the crowd before him, "your first clue, it says here, is where eggs mark the spot."

There was confused silence for a moment before the people in the crowd began murmuring to one another with furrowed brows. "Eggs?" They said to one another. "Eggs, or X?" A man cried out from the back of the crowd. "Did you say eggs?"

"Yes," the mayor called back, "where EGGS mark the spot. Not X, no, but eggs." He turned to his attendants. "That's right, isn't it? I don't want to get this wrong you know…."

"Oh, my word!" A lady in the front row suddenly screamed out. "I've got it!" And off she went, running down one of the cobbled lanes leading out of the town square.

"Oh, me too!" Another called out, dashing after her.

"Where are they going?" Said someone else.

"Oh, I know!" Said another, and ran after the others as fast as they could. Suddenly, there was uproar, as everyone - even those who had no idea what the first clue had actually meant - ran after them.

"Well, that's that then," the mayor said. "I do hope this was as good an idea as we hoped, you know…"

The crowd wound their way around the narrow lanes of the town, all following the people at the front who had apparently solved the first clue. People were dashing as fast as they can, leaping fences, running along the tops of walls, and even weaving among the crowd on bicycles, all in an attempt to win the race. At last, it became clear where they were all headed: just outside of the town, to Farmer Morgan's poultry sheds.

At the front of the crowd, the first woman was still in the lead. She turned the last corner, heading down to Farmer Morgan's field. Without thinking twice, she leapt over the farmyard gate, and ran across the chicken-filled field, over to the largest of the farmer's shed.

"Mr. Morgan!" She cried out, as she spotted the farmer standing by the shed door.

Behind her, the crowd of people following her was catching up and beginning to enter the field too.

"Goodness me!" Farmer Morgan shouted out when he saw the size of the group. "Just how many of them are you?! The mayor said nothing about anything like this!"

"The clue! The next clue!" the woman screamed. "Where is it?!"

Starting to panic as he saw just how many people were running across his land towards him, the farmer pointed at the chicken shed. "There! Good gracious! Over there!" And with that, he ran in the opposite direction, hoping not to be trampled in the commotion. Those at the front looked over and saw that pinned to the door of the chicken shed was another paper scroll, wrapped up in a yellow ribbon, just like the mayor's scroll.

"There!" Cried out one of the treasure hunters. "What does it say?!"

A man at the front of the crowd snatched the clue from the door before anyone else, unfurled it, and began reading it aloud. "You're not heading to the treasure yet - but here you might at least learn how to spell it."

"Spell it?" One man called out.

"Learn?" Another said.

"What does that mean?" Cried out a third.

More confused murmuring filtered through the crowd, until at last, one person called out, "Oh, I think I know!" and again they were off.

From Farmer Morgan's field, the crowd followed their new leader back up the hill, along the cobbled lanes, across the town square. "Lookout, here they come," the mayor said as he heard the crowd clamoring past and off to the opposite end of Easterburgh, where the local school was. And there, pinned to the door of the school library, was another scroll, tied up in yellow ribbon.

"There! On the door!" One lady shouted out.

"Grab the clue!" Screamed another.

A man at the front of the crowd tore down the scroll and untied the ribbon. But as the paper unfurled in his hand, he saw that this was not one sheet of paper, but five.

On one was written an E.

On another was written a P.

On a third was written an S, on a fourth an R, and the fifth an I.

"It's an anagram! A word jumble! A puzzle!" He cried out, as he placed the pages on the ground and began shuffling them around. A circle of people formed around him.

"RIPES?" One said, "what does that mean?"

"No, no, it's … PRISE?" Said another, not entirely convinced their answer was right.

"No, I've got it!" Called out another. "It must be … EPRIS? No, IRPES."

"Don't be so silly!" Called out another. "It's … SEPIR?"

Suddenly, the man who had held the scrolls gasped and looked up, and like that he was off, running back up towards the market square.

"Where's he going?" someone asked.

"He must know something," said another.

Another gasp and another person ran from the crowd, following the first.

"Where are they going?" Called out another.

"Oh, my word," said another, as he glanced down at the paper on the ground and the answer game to him. He looked up, over the roofs of the surrounding building, back up towards the market square, where the SPIRE of the local church towered above everything else around it.

"The church!" He called out.

Before long, the entire crowd was running back along the lanes to the market, jumping and scrambling over one another, desperately trying to be the first to get to the church.

Outside, the vicar was standing at the gate to the churchyard - but just like Farmer Morgan, when he saw the crowd barreling towards him, he hauled open the gate as wide as it would go, and, with a scream, ran off into the yard to escape being trampled.

"There!" Someone shouted, pointing up into the air. Above them, hanging just below the church spire, silhouetted against the Easter morning sky, was the mayor's golden egg, glistening in the sunshine. "In the bell tower!"

The crowd burst through the door of the church and ran up the winding spiral staircase that led up to the church bells. Round and round the stairs went, growing narrower and tighter as they went. The crowd was wild by now, with people pushing and shoving each other out of the way, all desperately trying to be the first to lay their hands on the grand prize.

Finally, they reached the top of the staircase, and the first man threw open the door to the very top of the spire. In front of him hung the large bells of the church - and hanging among them was the golden egg.

"There!" He shouted. But as he went to grab the egg, another person burst through the door behind him and knocked him off his feet, and together they both went clattering to the dusty wooden floor.

As more and more people entered the room, they all tumbled over the two men now scrambled to stand back up on the floor, until there was so many people writhing and struggling on top of one another that no one behind them could get in.

"Ow, my hand!" Someone shouted.

"That's my foot!" Another called out.

"Get off my back!" Another screamed.

Amid all the chaos, one lady finally found her feet again - but she was knocked backwards by another - which sent her clattering into one of the bells - which rang out as she hit it, and which - to everyone's horror - knocked into the golden egg!

The crowd gasped when they saw what had happened, as the egg swung loose from the string on which it was hanging and fell - not to the floor, but through the opening in it, down which the ropes used to ring the bells slunk down to the floor of the church downstairs.

"Oh no!" She cried as the egg disappeared from view, hurtling back down the way they had all come.

"Downstairs!" One man cried out.

"Quickly!" Shouted another.

Back on the ground floor of the church, of course, some people who had not been able to make it up the stairs to the bell tower, stood waiting to see who the winner was. Among them were the mayor and the vicar.

"I'm not sure this contest has gone quite to plan," the mayor said.

"I quite agree," said the vicar, "I've never seen such…."

And at that moment, a loud *bang* rang out around the church hall, as the golden egg crashed to the ground, having fallen the full length of the church spire.

"Merciful heavens!" The vicar cried out in shock, as he turned to find the mayor's golden egg shattered into hundreds of pieces on the stone floor of the church.

The crowd began to file down the stairs and walked somewhat sheepishly over to the broken egg.

"Wait," one person said.

"That's not gold…," said another.

"Gold?" Said the mayor, "well, when I said gold, I meant it's…."

"That's chocolate!" Called out another person from the crowd.

"A chocolate egg?" Said another.

The vicar stepped forward and picked up one of the shards of chocolate, still partly wrapped in glistening golden foil. He unwrapped it and took a bite.

"Mmm," he said, "that's good. In fact, that's delicious!"

"It was an Easter egg all along!" Shouted another, with a smile.

"A what?" Shouted someone.

Slowly, everything that had happened - and everything that they had been chasing so viciously all morning - began to dawn among the crowd, and laughter began to fill the church.

"An Easter egg!" One person laughed.

"All this for some chocolate?" Called out another.

"But it's very good chocolate!" One person shouted as people tipped a handful of the chocolate pieces into their mouth. "Very good!"

"And there's more than enough to go around!" Laughed the vicar, as he began handing pieces of the golden egg to everyone.

"Well," said the mayor, as the vicar handed him a piece of the egg, "things might have gotten a little out of hand, vicar," he laughed. "But at least this will be an anniversary we'll all remember!"

THE MAGIC KEY

Every Easter, Izzie and her best friend Charlie would spend a few weeks at Izzie's grandfather's house in the country.

It was an enormous old manor house, set in the middle of grassy fields and ornate gardens that stretched as far as the eye could see. Inside, it was full of winding corridors, wooden floors, stained glass windows, spiral staircases, and - as Izzie's grandfather had run an antique store for many years - room after room after room of quirky oddities and bizarre artifacts.

It was a truly magical place to be - the kind of rambling, ramshackle home where a wizard might live - and Izzie always imagined what kind of secrets lay hidden among its seemingly endless doorways and passageways.

She looked forward to her time there each year enormously. Having lived in the city all her life, it was a real treat to be out of the hustle and bustle of her neighborhood, and amongst the open fields and summer sunshine of her grandfather's home. For the past few years now, Charlie had come with her too and stayed at Izzie's grandfather's home with her during the holidays. The pair had been inseparable best friends since they had first joined the school and, like Izzie's parents, Charlie's mom often had to work away, leaving her at home during the holidays with only her aunty to keep her entertained. Her aunty was a lovely lady, Charlie would explain to Izzie, but she wasn't a lot of fun. She liked reading and sewing and watching television - boring things like that, Charlie said. But Charlie liked playing outside, climbing trees, and exploring the great outdoors, so the holidays staying with her aunt tended to drag. So, when Izzie had first invited Charlie along to stay at her grandfather's house, Izzie had understandably jumped at the chance - and now she enjoyed visiting Izzie's grandfather almost as much as Izzie herself.

"Now, you two behave," Izzie's mother said as she dropped the pair off outside on the first day of their Easter holidays. "And you too, dad," she said to Izzie's grandfather, standing beside her. "Make sure they don't get into any trouble. And no junk food, either. I know it's Easter, but I don't want them eating loads of chocolate and things...."

"Oh, don't worry," Izzie's grandfather replied with a smile, knowing full well that as soon as Izzie's mother's car was out of sight, the pair of them would already be running through the house, leaping over the bannisters, and out climbing trees in the garden as always. "You know you really do worry too much."

Izzie's mother gave her father a wry smile, and with that drove off back down the driveway. Izzie and Charlie waved as her car disappeared into the trees that led back down to the main road, and back to the city.

"Now," said Izzie's grandfather, clapping his hand together with glee. "How about I make us all some smores while you two go and get settled in?"

The rest of the day went exactly how Izzie and Charlie would have wanted it to. After unpacking their cases in their bedroom, the pair played outside in the spring sunshine all afternoon. And when the sun dropped down below the trees and it began to cool off, they brought their games inside and began exploring Izzie's grandfather's house from top to bottom. They poured over the endless books in his library. They made paper airplanes in his study and sent them spiraling down the grand staircase in the center of the house. And they made double chocolate milkshakes in his enormous kitchen and drank them out of the biggest paper straws they'd ever seen.

Izzie's grandfather showed them some of his latest purchases too. He had been an antique dealer all his life and had recently added an enormous old globe ("marked with countries and cities that haven't existed for years...," he laughed), along with an even older writing desk full of odd compartments and hidden drawers ("I like to think someone famous might once have owned it," he explained), and an old grandfather clock that stood proudly at the foot of the main stairs.

"Isn't it magnificent?" He said. He wound up the mechanism, and the clock swung magically into life. Izzie and Charlie watched its pendulum begin to swing gracefully back and forward, and all its cogs and dials whirred away softly inside. "I purchased this from a very curious fellow, I must say. An odd, stout sort of chap, who said it used to belong to his father - who apparently bought it long ago from another very curious fellow too, supposedly. I've no idea how old it is yet, but there's something quite remarkable about it - I've never seen a clock as grand as this in my life."

"Whoa!" Izzie said as she peered through the glass in the front of the clock's door, staring in amazement at all the gears and moving parts inside. "It's like an engine!"

"Ha, ha...!" Her grandfather laughed. "Well, I guess technically it is an engine," he explained. "You use this key to wind the mechanism up, and from there it runs and runs and runs."

The clock suddenly began to chime the hour, and a soft tinkling sound rang out through the house. "Ah!" Izzie's grandfather said, "well, you know what that means, you two. Time for bed. I'll see you in the morning. It's Easter Sunday tomorrow, and I'll need your help getting plenty of vegetables from the garden so we can make a lovely meal for ourselves."

That night, as they sat up in their bedroom, Izzie and Charlie were too excited to sleep. They kept each other awake by chatting back and forth about all the things they had seen and done on their first day at Izzie's grandfather's house, from spotting rabbits and butterflies in the gardens to the wonderful grandfather clock at the bottom of the stairs.

"Wasn't it amazing?" Izzie said.

"Did you see all the cogs and things inside?" Charlie replied. "I've never seen anything like it."

"Hey," Izzie said. "Come on. Let's take another look."

Charlie looked over at Izzie and smiled, and then the pair leapt silently out of bed and crept out of their bedroom, and back downstairs. There, the old clock was still whirring and ticking away in the moonlight shining down from the hall windows.

"Where's the key?" Izzie whispered. "Granddad said it needed winding with a key, but I can't see it."

The pair began looking around, on the tables and in the drawers of the furniture in the hallway, but they couldn't find the key to the clock.

"Wait," Charlie said, "maybe he kept it with him and took it up to his bedroom?"

"No," Izzie said. "I'm sure - wait...." She had had a brainwave. She walked back over to the clock, and carefully pulled open the glass door set in its front. "Let me see...," she muttered softly as she peered inside. Being careful not to touch any of the delicate workings inside, she felt around the wood frame of the clock until finally, she found it: hanging from a tiny hook on the inside of the clock case was a key. She took it out and examined it in the moonlight.

"Wait," she said, "this doesn't look like the one granddad had."

"No," Charlie agreed, "that was only small, and black. And it only had a couple of prongs on the end of it. That looks like it's made of brass or even gold, and..., well, it looks..."

"Like a door key!" Izzie interrupted.

The pair looked at one another and smiled. "But for what door?!" They said in unison.

Under cover of darkness, the pair began creeping around their grandfather's house, looking for anything with a lock big enough to match that of the bizarre gold key they had found hidden away inside the clock. It was difficult keeping quiet while on such an exciting quest, and it was even more difficult to search around such a gigantic house under cover of darkness, but after almost an hour of searching, the pair had found nothing. Defeated and yawning after a long and busy day, they decided to replace the key, and ask Izzie's grandfather about it the following morning.

As they crept back into the hallway, the grandfather clock was just striking midnight. "Happy Easter, Charlie!" She whispered with a laugh, as Easter Sunday had officially begun. As they walked over to the clock, though, Izzie noticed something that hadn't been there before. It appeared to be a light - a warm, bright yellow light - shining out from behind the clock case.

"What's that?" She asked.

"What's what?" Charlie replied, unaware.

"Over there, next to the clock," Izzie explained. Sure enough, as they walked closer, it became clear that besides the clock - outlining a panel in the wall of the hallway - was a square of golden light, like that that would shine out from behind a closed door.

"Is that...? Is that a doorway?" Charlie asked. "I didn't see that earlier, I'm sure."

"And is that ..., is that a keyhole?" Izzie replied, as they walked closer to the light and saw a separate, smaller circle of light just beside it. Cautiously, she placed the key in the hole and turned it. With a soft click, the secret lock released, and the square of light gradually grew as the door swung open, revealing a candlelit passageway behind it. The hallway was bathed in the warm glow shining out of the doorway as the girls pushed the door open the full way.

"A secret door?" Charlie said, astonished at what they were seeing. "But - but to where?"

"I guess there's only one way to find out," Izzie replied, and she stepped through the door and into the passageway behind it.

Together, the two girls followed the passage downwards, towards the source of the light. There were candles lining the full length of the passage, and a warm, sweet smell filled the air. Despite the cramped space - the girls could scarcely stand at their full height all the way down - it nevertheless felt like they were walking into a homely, welcoming place.

Finally, the passage turned sharply to the left and opened out into a small room. At one end was a stove, beside which was a small dresser, lined with plates and dishes. Next to that was a wooden table, a bookcase covered in books and papers, and a little bed with a red and white checkered blanket thrown over it. Finally, sat in front of a warm open fire, was a small green velvet armchair - in which sat a large rabbit.

As if that weren't bizarre enough, the rabbit appeared to be dressed in a small tweed coat, had a pair of spectacles perched on the end of its nose, and was sitting reading a book.

"What the…?" Izzie said.

"Aargh!" The rabbit shouted. "Oh, my word, you two startled me! You might at least have had the decency to knock, I could have …."

Suddenly, the rabbit stopped talking and noticed the key in Izzie's hand.

"Ohhh," he said knowingly, "you found the key, I take it? Well, come on in, come on in. Would you like some cocoa? I was just about to have some before I head out."

Izzie and Charlie stood open-mouthed, staring at the bizarre-looking creature that sat before them. "Or perhaps you would like to stand there and gawk at me all evening? I do have other places to go, you know, this is the busiest day of my year."

The two girls glanced at one another, open-mouthed, as the rabbit hopped down from its chair and crossed the room to the stove where a pot of hot chocolate was steaming gently.

"Well, come on, have a seat, have a seat!" The rabbit gestured to the table, beside which were a few wooden chairs. Still not saying anything, Izzie and Charlie walked across the room and sat down.

"I guess you know who I am, if you've found the key," the rabbit said as he poured out three small cups of cocoa.

"I—I mean, are you…?" Izzie began.

"No, surely… Is he?" Charlie answered.

Suddenly the rabbit took a golden pocket watch out of his coat and glanced at the time. "Oh, goodness. I have less time than I thought," he said as he handed the girls their drinks, and sat down opposite them at the table. "Tonight, is the night, of course," he said, as he began searching through his coat pockets as if checking that he had not forgotten anything.

"Now, drink up, you two," he said, "I really don't have time to waste. Do you have any requests, is that why you're here?"

"Here?" Izzie said. "Where exactly are we? Like, where is … here?"

Now it was the rabbit's turn to look dumbfounded. "You mean you really don't know? What day is it, my dear? And what do you think this is?"

As if from nowhere, the rabbit suddenly held a chocolate egg in his paws, and rolled it across the table to Izzie and Charlie. "Try it, try it! It's a new recipe we've been working on this year."

The egg had a thin red ribbon wrapped around it, which was tied in a bow. Izzie tugged at one of the bow's trailing tails, and as the ribbon unwound, the egg opened up, and two-dozen tiny multicolored candies spilt out across the tabletop.

"Ha, ha!" The rabbit laughed. "Quite the surprise, isn't it?"

Izzie and Charlie reached forward and placed one of the candies in their mouths.

"Oh, wow," Charlie said, "that's the nicest chocolate I've ever had!"

"Me too!" Izzie said, picking up another piece, and then breaking off part of the chocolate egg.

"Eat, eat!" The rabbit laughed. "It would only go to waste otherwise!"

The pair finished the chocolate and gulped the last of their cocoa, as the rabbit hopped over to a hook in the corner of the room and pulled a small red scarf around his neck. "This time of year," he muttered and turned to face the girls. "It's lovely during the day, but as soon as the sun goes down, oh my, does it get chilly! Are you all finished?"

The girls looked down at their drained cocoa cups. "Yes, thank you," Izzie said.

"That was delicious," Charlie added.

"Ah, you are most kind. Well, I'm afraid I have to go, for obvious reasons!" The rabbit said. "Come, come," he beckoned the girls over to the foot of the stairs again. "Back up the way you came - just follow the candles to the top, you can't miss it."

Izzie and Charlie began walking back up towards the hallway of the house. "Until we meet again," the rabbit called up behind them.

At the top of the stairs, the girls crawled back out of the passageway into the hall, and Izzie closed and locked the glowing door behind her. The light that had surrounded it slowly faded away, and all that was left was the key, the moonlight, and the ticking of the clock.

"Did that… did that *really* just happen?" She asked.

"I… I'm so tired, I really don't know," Charlie replied with a smile, as she wiped the chocolate off her lips. "I need to get some sleep!"

Izzie placed the key they had found back on the hook inside the clock, and together the pair crept back upstairs to bed.

The following morning, Izzie awoke to warm, bright spring sunshine flooding their room. Suddenly, there was a knock on the door. It was her grandfather.

"Girls?" He called from outside. "Izzie? Charlie? Are you awake?"

Izzie jumped down out of bed and headed over to the door, as Charlie began to stir. "What time is it?" she asked sleepily.

"Almost 8 o'clock," Izzie said, glancing at the clock that hung on the wall. She opened the door, to find her grandfather outside wearing an apron, with flour all over his hands and face, and holding two glasses of orange juice.

"Ah!" He said with a smile. "Good morning! Or rather, happy Easter! I've some freshly squeezed orange juice for you here, and once I can work out how to make them, there'll be some chocolate pancakes on the go downstairs in the kitchen too, when you're ready," he laughed.

He handed the glasses to Izzie, who gulped one of them. "Oh, that's delicious, thank you, granddad."

"My pleasure. See you both in a bit!" He said, and with that, he headed off downstairs again.

Izzie walked over to Charlie's bed and placed one of the glasses beside her. "Come on, sleepyhead," she said, as she walked back over to her bed and jumped back underneath the covers.

"Charlie," she said, "can you remember what happened last night? I still can't quite believe it."

"I know," Charlie muttered, seemingly still half asleep, "those paper planes flew for miles."

"No, no, not the planes!" Izzie shouted, throwing a pillow across the room at Charlie. "Wake up, will you! I mean the

57

rabbit! The clock! The key! The secret door! The cocoa, you know?"

Charlie turned over in bed and gave her friend a quizzical look. "The …, the what now? What on earth are you talking about?"

"What do you mean?" Izzie said. "You mean, you can't you remember? Any of it?"

"Remember what?" Charles replied. "I remember us talking, in here last night. Then…, then I remember…. Well, I must just have dropped off, I supposed. Boy, was I tired." She yawned and stretched as she sat up in bed. "Wait. The rabbit? The cocoa? Ha! What on earth are you talking about? Rabbits and keys and cocoa. What?!" Charlie laughed

"Well, I mean…," Izzie paused. "You really don't remember? Not one bit of it?" She said.

"No!" Charlie laughed. "What are you on about? Honestly, Izzie" she said as she jumped down out of bed and put on her dressing gown, "you get stranger every day, you really do. Rabbits and cocoa and keys. Whatever next!"

Charlie gulped down her orange juice. "Mm, that is delicious," she said. "And those pancakes your grandad is making smell even better. Come on, let's eat, I'm starved."

And with that, she scampered out of the room and headed down the stairs for breakfast. Izzie paused and sat for a moment in her bed.

"But …. But, I'm sure I didn't…," she muttered softly to herself. "Surely, it can't have all just been…."

Downstairs in the hallway, the grandfather clock chimed 8 o'clock.

"I was so sure…," Izzie continued, mutteringly to herself, as she hopped back out of bed, pulled on her slippers and, picking up her orange juice, headed downstairs for breakfast. "That really does smell delicious," she said as she walked out into the corridor outside, and smelled the aroma of chocolate pancakes drifting up the stairs. "Charlie's right, I'm absolutely starving."

In fact, she was so hungry that as she turned to the top of the stairs and began to skip down them into the hallway - keeping her eyes fixed on the grandfather clock at the bottom of them the whole time - she didn't even stop to notice the tiny red ribbon that fell out of her pajama pocket, and floated softly to the ground.

OLD MRS RATCLIFFE

Mrs. Ratcliffe was the meanest, nastiest, most unpleasant lady in town. Everyone knew it, too. Nobody liked her, and everyone avoided her.

What is more, the feeling was entirely mutual, because Mrs. Radcliffe disliked absolutely everybody else. Her house was a run-down old wooden frame building on the corner of Main Street and it looked out onto a crossroads, and Mrs. Radcliffe would spend most of her time sitting in her rocking chair by her window, glaring at anyone who dared to walk - or even drive-by.

And as for anyone who dared to set foot on her property, they had it worst of all. One day, for instance, a lady who was walking her little chihuahua dog stopped outside Mrs. Radcliffe's house to tie her shoelace - unaware that, as she did so, her little dog had wandered off, up the path to Mrs. Radcliffe's door, and begun sniffing around on her front lawn.

"GET THAT MANGY MUTT OFF MY GRASS!" Mrs. Radcliffe suddenly cried out, pounding her wrinkly hands against the dust-covered glass of her windows. "I DON'T TEND TO MY GARDEN JUST TO TURN IT INTO SOME KIND OF DIRTY TOILET FOR MANGY MUTTS!" She bellowed.

The woman out on the pavement jumped in shock and then saw where her dog had wandered. "Oh!" She exclaimed and began hauling the dog's leash back in, pulling it back down the garden path and out onto the pavement.

"WHAT AN UGLY-LOOKING DOG THAT IS TOO!" Mrs. Radcliffe shouted. "MORE LIKE A RAT THAN A DOG I'D SAY! HA! HA!" And with that, she began cackling and cackling, and fell back into her rocking chair, kicking her skinny legs up in the air with glee.

"Well, I never!" the woman replied, still a little flustered. "I…, well, I don't think it looks like you tend your garden at all, you mean old thing! Look at all those weeds and dead grass!" She replied, but it was no use. Mrs. Radcliffe couldn't hear anything over the sound of her cackling.

As anyone will tell you, though, the problem with being a mean person in a small town is that before long your meanness becomes known to everyone - even to people that don't know you. That weekend, the lady with the chihuahua dog had headed to church, and afterwards had started chatting and gossiping with everyone there about the nasty old lady who lived on the corner of Main Street.

"Oh, you mean Mrs. Radcliffe?" One of the other churchgoers had said to her. "Lives in the house down the road here, at the junction of Main Street? Mm-hm, you want to keep away from her."

"Is that her name?" The lady with the dog had said.

"Oh, yes, it is," another lady chimed in. "Ms. Adelia Radcliffe. She's lived in that tatty run-down old house for as long as I've been coming to this church - and heck, I've been here fifty years now!"

"She never leaves, she never goes anywhere, she never bothers with any of us," a third lady butted in. "I live a few doors down from her, across the crossroads on Main Street," she went on. "The year I moved in, I posted a getting-to-know-you card through her door, with my details on it, thinking we could be friends. She tore it right up and posted it back through my door the very next day!"

"Goodness me," the lady with the dog said, turning to her sister beside her. "Annie, did you hear this? That mean old lady that I was telling you about just the other day? Her name is Mrs. Radcliffe, and wait until you hear this…." And off they went together, chatting about everything they had heard.

And that, in a small town, is how gossip spreads - and how reputations, both good and bad, become known.

Even if Mrs. Radcliffe were not as mean and as nasty as she was, there were enough stories and tales about her odd behavior - and those stories were known to enough people across town - that there was no way she was ever going to be known as anything except a mean old lady.

But some people in town didn't quite want to believe everything they heard.

Also standing outside the church, alongside the gossiping ladies who were busy telling all their stories of mean old Mrs. Radcliffe, were two young friends, George and Allie. George was 9, and Allie was just about to turn 10, and the two had been friends for as long as they could remember.

"That old house on the corner," George said after he had heard the ladies talking, "the lady inside, she's called Mrs. Radcliffe?"

"Yeah," Allie answered. "I heard that too. Do you really think she's as nasty as they say she is?"

"I don't know," George said. "I really don't. Though I do remember a kid at school once said that his frisbee landed in the garden of that house, and just as he was walking up the path to get it back, the lady inside ran out laughing, and threw it far away, straight up in the air, way off over the tops of all the houses, and it drifted off somewhere into Potters' Forest. He never found it again, no matter how long he looked. He ended up having to ask his parents to get him a new one, I think."

"Really?" Allie said.

"That's what he said," George replied, shrugging his shoulders.

"Hm. I don't know, you know," Allie pondered. She was always the more thoughtful of the two, and like to find things out for herself rather than be told them. "I'm not so sure anyone would be that mean. At least, not for a reason."

That afternoon, Allie and George decided to investigate. They went out on their bikes in the spring sunshine and cycled the two blocks over from their road to the corner of Main Street. There, on the opposite side of the road from Mrs. Radcliffe's house, they sat on their bikes and looked across at her home.

"Can - can you see her?" Allie said nervously.

"No, I can't see anything through those windows," George answered, "they're filthy. And look at that garden! It's in a shocking state. Everyone else's garden is green and full of flowers this time of year. Hers is all dried out and full of weeks. The grass is brown, even."

"I wonder what she's really like," Allie muttered, "there must be a reason for it, you know. There's always a reason, for everything."

Just as they were standing talking, an ice cream truck pulled up at the Main Street junction and began to play its chiming song. Allie and George watched as the driver got down out of his seat, opened the hatch at the side of the van, and began shouting, "Ice creams! Ice creams! A lovely warm spring day like this, needs ice cream!"

A few children who were playing out down the street ran up to the van and began eagerly jumping up at the hatch. "Me, first! Me, first…," one of them shouted.

"Ha! ha!" The man inside laughed. "Alright then. What can I get you?"

Suddenly, the peaceful springtime scene was interrupted by a loud banging noise, and George and Allie watched as Mrs. Radcliffe stood at her window, pounding her hands against the glass.

"HEY!" She screamed. "YES YOU..., YOU FAT UGLY THING! GET THAT VAN AWAY FROM MY HOUSE!"

The ice cream man looked up at Mrs. Radcliffe, who glared back at him from inside her home.

"Wha..., *me*?" He stammered.

"YES YOU, YOU DUMB OAF!" Mrs. Radcliffe screamed back. "AND GET THOSE SNOTTY KIDS AWAY FROM MY FENCE! TAKE YOUR ROTTEN OLD VAN AND ITS ROTTEN OLD MUSIC AND BEAT IT!"

The ice cream man stared back, quite unable to believe what he was hearing. "Well, I never! How dare you!" He shouted back.

"HOW DARE I? OH, I DARE *YOU*!" Mrs. Radcliffe bellowed. "I DARE *YOU* TO GET LOST!" She screamed with her usual cackling laugh.

"Now, listen here, you mean old sow...," the man shouted back, "it's a hot day out here, and these kids want ice creams. This is a public street, and I'm going to sell them ice creams on it, whether you like it or not! And you can't do anything about it, you rotten old witch!"

George and Allie looked at one another. They had the uncomfortable feeling that this wasn't going to end well.

"OHH, IT'S LIKE THAT IS IT?" Mrs. Radcliffe shrieked back from inside. "FINE!"

Suddenly, she disappeared from the window. "Hmph!" the ice cream man said. "That saw her off, didn't it? Now," he went on, turning back to the half-dozen kids who were now standing at his hatch. "You, son, what can I get you?"

Just at that moment, the door to Mrs. Radcliffe's home burst open, and out she strode. She was dressed head to toe in black, wore big leather books that seemed to lace halfway up her legs, and had her dark black hair pulled back in a tight bun at the back of her head. Her face was a picture of pure rage.

She stormed out onto her porch, pushing past pots of dead and dried-up old flowers and plants, and hauled an ancient-looking garden hose off the wall. "CAN'T DO ANYTHING ABOUT IT?" She screamed again.

The ice cream man looked up, his first customer's ice cream still in his hand. "What the...."

But it was too late. Mrs. Radcliffe turned her hose on full blast, and a stream of ice-cold water shot across her garden, over the top of her tatty old fence, and into the hatch of the ice cream van, soaking the man inside and sending the children outside running and screaming down the road. Mrs. Radcliffe cackled with delight as she turned off the hose.

The ice cream man wiped the water from his face. "Why, you, horrible scrawny old crone!" He shouted.

"OH, SAVE IT FOR SOMEONE WHO CARES!" Mrs. Radcliffe bellowed back and stormed back in her house.

"Why - why, you tired out old toad! You, spindly old spinster!" Shouted the ice cream man. Mrs. Radcliffe reappeared at her window and began cackling all over again when she saw the drenched man still standing at the hatch of his van. "Oh, why don't you do us all a favor," he screamed, "get yourself out of our town, you old crow! Go and fly back to your nest, you... you rotten old magpie!"

Mrs. Radcliffe stopped laughing and glared even harder out of the window.

"Go and do one!" The ice cream man yelled back. "And by 'do one', I mean throw yourself off a pier!"

"BAH!" Mrs. Radcliffe screamed and yanked her living room curtains closed. And with that, the ice cream man sped off down the street again, as his jangling tune faded into the distance.

"Still think there's a reason for all this?" George asked Allie doubtfully. "She sure seems just like a mean old lady to me."

"Well," Allie said. "Maybe she's mean because everyone is mean to her, you know?"

"I don't think I do," George said.

"Listen," Allie said. "I've got a plan. Remember, it's Easter this weekend. That doesn't give us long. We need to spread the word at school tomorrow. Come on."

And with that, she and George cycled back off down the street.

The following weekend, it was Easter Sunday, and as usual most of the town had turned out in their finery to attend the Easter service at the church. Afterwards, everyone was milling around in the churchyard, chatting and catching up in the warm spring sunshine. George and Allie were standing with as many as two dozen of their friends from school.

"So," Allie said. "Did you all bring one?"

Everyone nodded.

"Okay," Allie continued. "Let's go, while no one is looking."

Altogether, the twenty or so children from Allie and George's class set off out of the churchyard, and off down Main Street.

"Children?" A voice called out behind them. It was Mrs. Sanderson, their teacher. "Children, where are you going?"

But the kids didn't look back, and just kept on walking.

"Children? Children!" Mrs. Sanderson called out, more loudly than before. A few other people in the churchyard turned to see what the fuss was. But the kids all kept walking.

"Now, what are they up to?" Mrs. Sanderson muttered, and followed them out of the churchyard and off down the street, with a number of the other grown-ups following close behind.

Meanwhile, Allie, George, and the rest of the kids had arrived at Mrs. Radcliffe's house. There was no sign of her.

"Here goes nothing," Allie said, as she pushed open her garden gate and the children all began to file up to her door.

Allie reached into the pocket of her coat and pulled out some sheets of colored paper and a chocolate egg she had picked up from the store the previous day. Behind her, George took another chocolate egg from his pocket. And behind him, so too did the rest of the children. One by one, they filed up to Mrs. Radcliffe's door, where Allie had set down the paper on the boards of the porch—making a little paper nest for her chocolate - and one after the other, they placed their chocolate eggs into it. Once all twenty of them were in place, Allie took a deep breath and rang Mrs. Radcliffe's doorbell.

The children all ran back down the garden path and waited nervously at the gate. After a few seconds, the door swung open and Mrs. Radcliffe stood there in the sunshine.

"YOU LOT!" She bellowed. "HOW MANY TIMES DO I …."

As she took a step outside, the toe of Mrs. Radcliffe's boot knocked against the paper nest on the floor, and she looked down at the pile of chocolate gifts the children had left her. "What on earth…," she muttered, "are those…?"

She looked up and saw Allie and the other children smiling nervously at her. Allie still wasn't quite sure whether her plan was going to work, and half expected Mrs. Radcliffe to stamp the heel of her book down into the chocolate eggs and run cackling back into the house. But she didn't.

Instead, she slowly crouched down, and picked up one of the eggs, and looked at it curiously, almost as if she'd never had a gift nor seen anything like it before. The silver foil that the egg was wrapped in glistened in the sunshine.

"Well, I'll be," she said to herself. She looked back up at the kids, who were smiling more broadly now. "For me?"

Allie nodded slowly. "For you, Mrs. Radcliffe. Happy Easter."

For a moment, Mrs. Radcliffe said nothing. She seemed lost for words as if finding herself for the first time in a situation where names and insults were useless. "Well," she said finally. "Thank you. All of you. Thank you, this... this is very unexpected." Her voice was soft and low, not at all like the bellowing yell Allie and George had heard earlier.

By this point, the people from the churchyard had arrived and were dumbstruck by what they had seen and heard. At the front of the ground was Mrs. Sanderson.

"Good .... Good morning, Mrs. Radcliffe," she ventured, "Happy Easter."

Mrs. Radcliffe said nothing but nodded graciously. More and more people were arriving now. "Happy Easter," another voice called out.

"Happy Easter, Mrs. Radcliffe," said another.

She nodded again. "Happy Easter, all of you," she said softly. "Well, now," she went on, looking up at the children at her gate. "I couldn't possibly eat all of these chocolates on my own. Perhaps you'd all like to come in for some tea?"

A VOYAGE TO EASTER ISLAND

On a farm in the countryside, far away from the nearest towns and cities, lived a family of rabbits.

Not that this was any ordinary family, of course. This was an extended family - a huge mishmash of mothers and fathers, sons and daughters, grandsons and granddaughters, aunts and uncles, cousins, nieces, nephews, and friends. The entire group lived together in a vast warren, full of interconnecting burrows and tunnels that seemed to run for miles and miles below the ground in a long stretch of woodland running down the entire lefthand side of the farm. On the opposite side, running down the entire righthand side of the farm, was a huge lake, whose waters seemed to go on forever, as far as the eye could see.

On the whole, life in the woods was perfectly peaceful. The trees kept the rabbits dry when it rained, kept them cool in the summer, and kept them sheltered when it snowed or was windy. But under the shade of the trees, out of the way of the sun and the rain, the grass and the flowers on which the rabbits fed never grew particularly tall or green. So, whenever they got hungry (which happened a lot - these were rabbits, after all!), they all had to venture out into the open fields of the farm.

There, a feast was waiting for them. The grass on the farm was fresh and bright green, and entirely delicious. In some of the fields, too, the rabbits had found that the farmer was growing huge leafy vegetables, like cabbages and lettuces and carrots, that were even nicer than the grasses and weeds of the fields.

But venturing out into the open fields and onto the farmer's land came at a cost. The farmer was notoriously bad tempered and understandably didn't much like the fact that the rabbits from the woods would munch away at his crops whenever his back was turned. And as a result, he had concocted all kinds of schemes to keep the rabbits at bay and keep them away from his crops.

First, he had erected an enormous fence that ran around the entire edge of his land - but the rabbits had dug their way under it, and forced their way through the holes and gaps in its posts and wires. Second, he had tried planting his vegetables in tall, raised flowerbeds, in enormous wooden crates full of soil, that sat high above the ground. But so determined were the rabbits to reach the food inside, that they had again simply leapt and clambered up into the crates and continued their meal. Thirdly and finally, as a last resort, the farmer adopted four huge dogs from the farm next door. And this last tactic had worked very well indeed.

Now, every time the rabbits dared to venture out of the woods and onto the farmer's land, the dogs would be onto them immediately, barking loudly and chasing after them, and forcing them to dash for cover back under the trees and in their tunnels. Day by day, what had once been an easy life of lying in the sun and eating lettuces and cabbages and carrot leaves, was now becoming increasingly unpleasant.

"We have to do something!" One of the rabbits said one day. "These dogs are ruining our quiet little lives here on the farm!"

"But what can we do?" Asked another. "The dogs are bigger than us. They're louder than us. Some of them are even faster than us! What can we do?"

"Well, I'm not going anywhere," said another of the rabbits, "I was born on the farm. My parents were born on the farm. My grandparents were born on the farm. This is my home, and if I have to put up with some troublesome dogs to continue living here then so be it."

"I'm inclined to agree…," muttered another of the rabbits contemplatively, munching on a carrot stalk that he'd run back to the woods with.

"Me too," said another, her mouth still full of cabbage leaves.

"And me," said a third, as he lay snoozing in the sunlight shining down through the trees.

"Well, I'm not," said another. A young rabbit hopped forward into the middle of the group and looked around at everyone. "There must be somewhere better than this," he continued. "Somewhere with no dogs and no farmers. Just fresh grass, as far as the eye can see, with nothing to worry about at all."

"That sounds perfect to me," said another young rabbit who sat nearby, idly scratching his ear.

"Doesn't it just?" Said another, as she bounded excitedly up to the group.

"Bah!" Said one of the older rabbits. "There's no such place. You, youngsters, daydream too much."

"Quite right," said another, who was standing beside him, "you're daydreaming, all of you. There's nowhere like that around here. Around *anywhere*, I bet."

The young rabbits all looked at one another disappointedly. "Hmm…" came a deep voice from somewhere in the distance. "That may be where you're wrong."

The rabbits turned to see one of the eldest of all their group - a huge old grey rabbit, whom they all knew and all looked up to - totter slowly up out of one of the tunnels, and sit himself down on the cool soil. "I've heard of just such a place. A long, long time ago now, of course, but there's a place out there."

"Oh, now, don't go telling your stories," said another rabbit wearily, she was an old, pale-furred female, who was almost as old as he was.

"No, no," said the old rabbit again, "you know what I'm talking about. Easter Island."

"Easter Island?" Said one of the young male rabbits. "Is that where…?"

"Where the Eater Bunny lives, yes, yes," said the old female rabbit, as she rolled her eyes. This was a story she had heard a great many times before. And she didn't believe a word of it.

"Where is Easter Island?" Asked another of the young rabbits, his long ears standing on end so he could hear.

"Oh, it's far, far away, way off across the sea," said the old male rabbit wisely. "But it's a real place, I tell you. No matter what anyone says. And it's perfect for a young rabbit like yourself. Full of fresh, long, green grass. Lots of warm sunshine. Cool air. And absolutely no dogs. And definitely no farmers."

The wise old rabbit's story had attracted the attention of around half a dozen of the young rabbits, who all looked at one another excitedly and began bounding around him excitedly. "That sounds perfect!" One of them said.

"Absolutely!" Said a second.

"We're going to meet the Easter Bunny!" Said a third.

The old female rabbit wearily rolled her eyes again. "Now, now," she said, "don't go getting yourselves too excited. How on earth are you going to find your way across miles and miles of open ocean - let alone across the farm, and past the dogs?" But her warning was too late. The young rabbits were all now too excited and were bounding around one another chattering excitedly - and planning their trip to Easter Island.

The next day, the young rabbits woke early and met by the edge of the woods.

"Right," said the young male who had organized them. "Is everyone here? We have a long trip ahead of us if we're going to make it to Easter Island today. So, let's go and grab some breakfast, and fill ourselves up so we have enough to last us until we get there." And together, they bounded off towards the bottom end of the farm, where the farmer was growing his latest crop of carrots. The two old grey rabbits watched as they scampered off into the long grass.

"You know," said the old female, "you really shouldn't fill their heads with such nonsense..."

The old grey male chuckled to himself. "Oh, no, it's not nonsense, and you know it." He turned to the female beside him, "and I've got a good feeling they're all going to know it soon too."

At the bottom end of the farm, the young rabbits were busy gobbling as many carrots as they could. But their peaceful breakfast wasn't too last, as before long there was a shout from the farm, the sound of a door being thrown up, and the loud barking of the dogs.

"Quick!" Shouted one of the rabbits. "Run!"

Together, the young rabbits leapt among the carrot plants and sprinted off towards the other side of the farm.

"Where are we going?" Shouted one of them.

"Shouldn't we be going back to the woods?" Shouted another, as the barking grew louder behind them.

"This way!" Shouted the leader. "Into the long grass!" And off he went, zigzagging into the vast open field in front of the farmhouse, disappearing into the long yellow grass and leaving the woods far behind him. "Quickly!" He shouted after him.

The other rabbits followed after him, running and running and running as fast as their legs could take them. Behind them, the sound of the barking gradually stopped, as the dogs became confused by the rabbit's sudden disappearance. They sniffed and sniffed the ground, trying to track down their scent, but their zigzagging route had confused them and the dogs ran off in the wrong direction, barking loudly again and heading back upwards towards the farmhouse.

The rabbits watched, hidden from view among the long grass, as the dogs disappeared and their barking drifted off into the distance.

"Phew!" One of them said. "That was close!"

"Too close!" Said another, his mouth still full of carrots.

"They ruined my breakfast," said a third, "I could have stayed there all day."

"Don't worry about your breakfast!" Shouted the young male rabbit. "We'll have more than enough to eat where we're going. Come on, this way!"

And off he went again, scampering as fast as he could possibly go. The other rabbits followed, leaving the woods ever further behind them.

Eventually, the long grass began to thin out, the wind began to strengthen, and the earth beneath the rabbits' feet became damp and silty. They looked up as ahead of them - as far as the eye could see - was a huge expanse of water.

"Look!" Yelled the young male rabbit excitedly. "The sea! Easter Island must be somewhere out there!"

The other rabbits weren't convinced. They looked at one another uncertainly and looked down at their muddy paws. "I'm not so sure," one of them muttered.

"I don't know...," said another.

"I want to go and finish my breakfast," said a third.

But the young male rabbit was having none of it. "Quick," he said as he scampered up and down the edge of the lake, splashing the muddy water up onto his front. "We need to figure out how we're going to get there. It'll be too far too swim; we need a boat."

"A boat?" Scoffed one of the other rabbits. "And just how do you expect us to find....?"

But again, it was too late. The young male rabbit had spotted something and was off, racing up the side of the lake.

"Hey!" Shouted one of the others. "Wait up!" and off she ran, after him.

"Wait for me!" Said another a moment later, and off he ran too.

"Oh, this better be worth it," said a third as he chased after them. "I still want some more breakfast."

Further up the lakeside, the young rabbit had spotted something even the farmer had long forgotten about. Lying in the mud and the damp grass was an old wooden barn door, which the previous winter had come crashing down during a storm and blown across the farmer's field, leaving broken timbers and panels scattered all across it. What was left here by the waterfront scarcely resembled a door - but it was just large enough and flat enough to prove the perfect size for half a dozen rabbits.

"Here! Help me drag it to the water!" The young rabbit shouted, and he leapt up onto the bank and pushed the barn door down the slope with all his might. The other rabbits soon joined him, and together they hauled the door to the lakeside, where it was picked up by the waves and began to drift away from the shore, just like a raft.

"Quickly!" He shouted. "Jump on!"

Before the door could drift too far from the bank, the rabbits scrambled their way on top of it, soaking their fur and splashing their faces as they went. As the last rabbit leapt on top, he pushed their makeshift raft as strongly as he could, and it slowly and steadily drifted out into the middle of the lake.

"So, which way to Easter Island?" Said one of the rabbits.

"I can't see anything, anywhere at all," muttered another, scanning the horizon.

"I'm not so sure this is a good idea…," said a third.

But the young male was convinced. "No! It's out there somewhere, I just know it is!" he said firmly. He hopped over to the front of the barn door and stood looking out across the water of the lake. He smiled. The door bobbed up and down gently as it drifted across the lake. "We just need to wait."

As the day wore on and the spring sun rose higher and higher into the sky, the raft slowly floated its way further and further from the shore, further from the farm, and further from the woods. Still, the young male rabbit stood at the front of it, looking out across the lake, utterly convinced that Easter Island lay somewhere ahead of them. But as the minutes - and then the hours - ticked by, the others were becoming worried.

"I'm hungry!" One of them said.

"It's too hot!" Complained another.

"I think we should go back...," muttered a third.

"I...," began a fourth, until something caught his eye. "What's that?" He said. Slowly and carefully, looking straight ahead, through narrowed eyes, out across the lake, he walked to the front of the raft. Something had caught his eye. "Do you see...?"

But the young male had already seen it. Way off in the distance, something green was beginning to appear on the horizon. And as the boat continued to drift forwards, it grew larger and clearer. "Is that...?" He said.

"An island!" Shouted another, jumping excitedly in the air. "It's an island!"

Sure enough, out in the middle of the lake, a large island slowly came into view. It was large - much larger than it had originally appeared - and as the raft slowly bobbed towards it, the rabbits could see that it was covered in long, lush, bright green grass. At one end was a huge grove of tall willow trees, whose tangly roots had risen from the earth, forming holes and tunnels that looked perfect for burrows. The trees' leaves drooped gracefully down into the water - providing plenty of cool shade out of the heat of the sun.

Eventually, the rabbit's raft drifted right up to its shore, nudged its way through the drooping willow branches, and settled in the wet earth beneath them. One by one, the rabbits hopped off it, and onto dry land, and slowly wandered out from below the willow trees. Ahead of them lay a huge expanse of the freshest, greenest, coolest grass they had even seen. And amongst it, grew patches of weeds and wildflowers, which buzzed with life as bumblebees and hoverflies zipped back and forth in the sunshine. There was not a dog, nor a farmer, anywhere to be seen.

"Easter Island," the young male rabbit muttered to the others. And leaving the raft moored by the shore below the trees behind them, together they hopped off into the grass.

THE TREE AT THE EDGE OF THE FOREST

One warm Easter morning, Ally and her brother Lucas were out walking their dog Rosie in the woods next to their home. Suddenly, Rosie caught sight of something in the undergrowth, dashed off into the bushes by the side of the path and vanished from sight.

"Hey!" Lucas called out after him, but it was no use. Rosie was already far, far out of sight.

"Oh, no," Ally muttered. "Lucas, I think she's seen a rabbit. Look!" She pointed into the ferns and grasses by the side of the path, as another rabbit scampered by. "Oh, we need to get her back! Quick, Lucas, after her!"

Together they ran after Rosie, following her excitable barking and panting, and the sound of the bushes and ferns ahead of them being crushed under her paws. As they ran, the trees grew thicker and the sunlight overhead became dim until Ally and Lucas could barely make their way forwards without pushing through a dense mesh of twigs, branches, and leaves.

"Are you sure this is the way she came?" Lucas called out behind Ally, as she pushed her way forward.

"Sure," she replied - though if she was honest, she wasn't entirely sure.

Suddenly, the trees ahead became sparse, and Ally was able to quicken her pace as the warm spring sunlight began to filter through the leaves. Finally, she and Lucas burst out of the trees and found themselves standing in a lush, grassy, sunlit clearing right by the very edge of the forest just in time to catch sight of a rabbit dashing off into the long grass. And there, at the very edge of the clearing, where the fence surrounding the forest backed out onto the farms and fields behind it, sat Rosie - looking quizzically up at one of the most bizarre trees Ally and Lucas had ever seen.

"Look at this place!" Ally exclaimed. "Lucas, are you seeing this?"

"Whoa!" Lucas said, as he strode forward into the sunshine and felt the soft, thick grass beneath his feet.

Rosie turned around, her tongue lolling out of her mouth, and gave a cheery bark.

"Rosie!" Ally scolded. "Bad girl!" Rosie dropped her head and walked sheepishly over to Ally, and gave her an apologetic nudge on her leg. "You know better than to run off like that, never do - wait." Ally stopped. "What are you looking at?"

Rosie was now sat beside Ally, snuggled in against her leg, but had her eyes fixed upwards, staring into the branches of the tree.

Ally looked upwards, to where Rosie too was looking and gasped.

"What? What is it?" Lucas said. "What are you….?" Now, it was his turn to gasp.

Far above their heads, the branches of this grand tree looked to be covered in enormous chocolate eggs. Bough after bough after bough, eggs of every size were nestled among the tree's leaves, some sitting proudly upright, others seeming to hang down, suspended from the branches.

Lucas ran forward, jumped up to one of the lower limbs, and grabbed one of the eggs from the branch. "Mm!" He said as he took a bite. "Ally, these are delicious!" Ally - with Rosie running excitedly behind her - ran forward, and joined her brother in taking an egg from the branches.

"Oh, you're right!" She said as she took a bite of the chocolate. "Here, help me fill my bag!"

Ally opened the buckle on her backpack, and together she and Lucas began filling it, their pockets and their arms with as many eggs as they could manage. Once there was no more room, Ally carefully fastened her back again making sure not to crush any of the eggs inside, and together she, Lucas, and Rosie trudged back through the trees and the undergrowth and headed up to the path.

Back home, Ally and Lucas' parents could scarcely believe what they were saying.

"Now, look here," their father said as he peered quizzically over the top of his morning newspaper. "A tree that grows chocolate eggs? You guys know better than that, now don't tell tales."

"But we're not!" Lucas shouted.

"Look!" Ally added, opening her back to show her dad what was inside - a pile of broken chocolate eggs, shattered and partly melted to pieces.

Her dad laughed. "Ha, ha! Oh no, now come on, what have you done with all the Easter eggs your mom and I gave you? They're all smashed to pieces."

"But dad! They're not those eggs, we found these on that tree…."

But Ally and Lucas' dad just shook his head dubiously and went back to his paper.

Ally sighed. "Come on Lucas," she said, and off they went to the kitchen to unpack the shards of chocolate eggshell from her bag.

The rest of the day, all they could talk about was their discovery of the bizarre tree at the edge of the forest - and with no one willing to believe them, Ally and Lucas decided to head back into the forest and down to the clearing again the next morning to collect more eggs. Unfortunately, their plan didn't quite work out.

The following morning, back Ally, Lucas, and Rosie went down the woodland path - back to where they had Rosia had caught site of the rabbit - and again headed off back through the undergrowth, then through the thickets and trees, until they reached the clearing. Again, the sun shone down at the very edge of the forest. And again, Rosie ran over to the fence, with the open farmland and fields behind it running off into the distance. And again, there was the tree, which Rosie sat looking at, staring intently up into its branches. Only this time, something was different.

Ally and Lucas looked up at the tree, and saw that its branches were no longer lined with chocolate eggs. Instead, hanging from every branch, and nestled between almost every leaf from the lowest boughs to the very top of the tree, were countless toy bones. Rosie looked overjoyed.

"Bones!" Lucas said. "Toy bones? What happened to the eggs?"

"Wait, that - that doesn't make sense, I…," Ally stammered. "I…, where are the eggs?"

The two looked at one another, as Rosie suddenly spotted one of the bones, then another, and then yet another, and began jumping and leaping up at the tree excitedly trying to snatch one of them from its branches.

"Come on," Ally said, opening her bag, "we've come this far…."

Together, she and Lucas once more filled up her bag - though not this time with chocolate eggs, but with countless toy bones. Rosie could hardly be more excited and was leaping and bounding around excitedly the entire time. When her bag could fit no more bones, Ally fastened the buckle, threw it back onto her back, and turned to take one more look at the tree.

"I guess it was only Easter for one day, after all," Lucas said.

"Yeah, I guess so…," Ally replied, as together they head back into the vegetation, heading back up to the path.

Behind them, the rabbit Rosie had chased peered out from behind the tree and watched them leave. Then, just as it had the previous day, it hopped off into the long grass and disappeared into the undergrowth.

EASTER IN THE SUN

Far away, in the middle of the ocean, was a tiny tropical island.

The island was so small that there was only one town - more of a village, really - that was home to everyone who lived there. But that's not to say that *nothing* lived outside of the village. In fact, quite the opposite. The island was full of life and was home to countless birds and animals that lived all over it - on its beaches, among its trees, in its lakes, and in its fields.

One spring morning, the animals on the island awoke to find they had a visitor. An enormous albatross had landed on the island overnight and was sitting in the middle of a grassy field by the beach, snoozing quietly in the sunshine. Many of the other animals had only ever heard of an albatross before, and had never seen one - so to have one very unexpectedly visit their island was quite an event. As it snoozed, the other animals gathered around it, looking quizzically at this unusual sight.

Suddenly, the albatross woke up, and finding himself surrounded by other birds and mice and snakes and lizards and all manner of other animals, he leapt up into the air in fright.

"What! What! What!" He spluttered, as he landed back down on the grass with a clumsy thump. "What is the meaning of this?! Can't a bird snooze in peace these days?! I've had a very long journey here, you know, you can't just go sneaking up on an albatross like this, this is most irregular!"

"Oh no!" Exclaimed a badger who was standing nearby. "We didn't mean to startle you, Mr. Albatross! We've just never seen a bird quite like you, before."

"Oh," the albatross muttered, preening his feathers, and standing proudly upright before them, "well, yes, I suppose I am quite a sight if you're not used to me," he chuckled.

"Where... Where have you come from?" Asked a quiet little bear cub.

"Yes, where have you flown from?" Asked a rabbit, as it bounded out of the long grass and up to the albatross' feet.

"Oh, I have flown here from far, far away," the albatross said, "far away, out across the sea, over the other side of the equator."

"The... equator?" Asked a somewhat confused-looking raccoon, as it trotted up to the other animals and sat beside the rabbit.

"Yes, yes, yes!" Exclaimed the albatross. "Far out there, across the equator. On an island most, most unlike this one."

"Wow!" Shouted a fox, as it too walked up and joined the group. "What kind of island?"

"Oh, much colder and wetter and windier than this one, I'm afraid to say," the albatross chuckled, "a most peculiar place. But the people there are just as kind as the people who live in around here."

"Really?" Asked the badger.

"Oh, yes," the albatross said, and he began telling the animals all about the odd, cold, wet little island he had just arrived from. He told them all about cars and trucks. About supermarkets and motorways. About airplanes and airports. He told them about factories, chimneys, bridges, and flyovers. He told them about office blocks and apartment blocks. About the summer holidays and school holidays. About Christmas and St Valentine's Day. And last of all, all about Easter.

"So that happens every spring?" Asked the fox.

"Oh, yes," the albatross said wisely, "every year. It's this week, in fact, in the spring."

"And, it's really all organized by a rabbit, just like me?" Asked the young rabbit, who had sat amazed at the albatross' stories.

"Yes, yes," the albatross said, "just like you. The Easter Bunny. He won't visit here, I'm afraid, it's too far away for him. But he's out there, back on that other island, handing out his eggs to all the children and families."

"He doesn't have to come here," the rabbit said, "I mean, I'm a bunny. And as you say, it's is nearly Wester."

"Easter," the albatross said, chuckling at the rabbit's mistake. "Well, yes, I suppose you are, you're right."

"Are you thinking what I'm thinking?" Said the raccoon.

"Are *you* thinking what *I'm* thinking?" Asked the badger in return.

"Is who thinking what about what?" Exclaimed the albatross. But the other animals were already huddled around him, excitedly going over their new plan.

****

A few days later, the animals were ready to put their plan into action. Early, on what the albatross had told them was Easter morning, they gathered in the field by the village. The previous night, the raccoon and the fox had crept into the village and collected a dozen eggs from the chickens kept by the people who lived there, and the animals had spent the night coloring them as best they could with what they could find around them. The albatross stood in the morning sunshine, looking over the animals' work.

"Hmm…," he said unconvincedly, "I know I told you that the Easter eggs are usually brightly colored, but these…?" He bent down and pecked at one of the eggs, which the badger and the fox had spent the night coating in thick orangey mud, and sticking grass and flower petals too.

The badger looked down at his messy paws. "We did the best we could, Mr. Albatross," he said.

"And in fairness," added the fox. "It was dark."

The albatross gave them an unsure look from the corner of his eyes and shrugged his wings. "Very well, my friends," he said. "I shall watch with interest how your plan goes." And with that, he took a run along the grassy beach and leapt up into the air. The animals watched below as he soared higher and higher above the island, cawing as he went.

"Right," said the rabbit. "Each of you - take an egg. Let's go." Together, the animals picked up one egg each, and with their precious cargo bundled up into their arms and paws, they slowly crept, crawled, waddled, and walked their way into the village.

It was still early morning, so the village was still quiet when they arrived. "We're going to have to be very quiet," the rabbit whispered, "because we don't want to be discovered. Remember, the Wester Bunny does everything while everyone is asleep."

The badger rolled his eyes. "Easter, not Wester!" The badger hissed - but the rabbit didn't hear, as he had already hopped ahead to the first house.

"So," he said, "the plan is that we need to sneak one egg into every house. That way, they'll all know the Wester Bunny has been. How exciting!"

This time, it was the turn of the raccoon to roll his eyes. "*Easter!*" He hissed. "*Easter, Easter*. Stop saying Wester!"

"What?" The rabbit replied, perking his ears up so that he could hear.

"Bah!" The raccoon shouted angrily, and in a quick leap, he jumped up onto the porch of the first house, and then up onto one of its windowsills so the rabbit could hear him. "Easter, I said! Easter!" He shouted down at the rabbit. "Stop saying, Wester!"

"Shhh!" The other animals hissed - but it was too late. From inside the house, there was a sudden commotion, a loud crash as of something heavy falling over, and a scream.

"Aaargh!" The voice yelled out. "Raccoon!"

Sat on the windowsill, the raccoon turned to peer into the house when suddenly the brushy head of a broom was thrust through the window. "Get away!" The voice inside called out, screaming again. "Aaargh! Raccoon!"

Knocked off the windowsill by the broom, the raccoon tumbled to the floor of the porch and landed with a splat - right on top of his egg.

"Oh, no!" he called out. The other animals fled to the next house as the screaming and commotion inside the first continued. The raccoon picked himself up, quickly wiped the egg off his fur, and scampered down to join the others. Up in the air, far above, the albatross was cawing with laughter.

At the second house, the rabbit again took charge. "Well," he said to the others. "That was a disaster. Let's see if we can do better here - ratty, now it's your turn."

The animals all turned to the rat, who picked up his egg and hopped up the steps to the front of the next house and peered inside.

"Good!" The rabbit called after him. "Now - careful. Sneak inside and leave the …."

But it was no use. From inside the house, a scream called out again. "Aaargh!" the person inside called out. "A rat! A rat!" Then, another voice and another scream. "Aargh! Fetch the broom!" And then, another broom came barreling out of the front of the house, knocking the poor rat sideways, and sending him and his egg tumbling down the front steps onto the ground. The animals scattered and fled for the third house as the rat's egg cracked open and spilt out onto the soil, and the screams faded into the distance. And way above their heads, the albatross cawed and cawed with laughter.

At the third house, the rabbit was determined the plan was going to work. "Right, this time," he said, "I'll handle things. Bear, pass me your egg, will you?"

The bear strode forward, gently nudging his precious egg along the ground, and joined the rabbit at the front of the house. "Here you …."

But again, it was too late. From somewhere inside of the house, another scream. Then another. Then a third. "Bear!" Screamed the first.

"Bear!!" Screamed the second, louder than before.

"BEAR!!!" Screamed the third.

Even in the house next door, another scream went up. "Did you hear?" Someone called out. "There's a bear in the village!"

From house to house, one scream followed another, and windows and doors were slammed shut and the people inside barricaded themselves indoors. In all the commotion, the animals didn't know which way to turn, and in the end, dropped all their eggs on the ground, and ran off back to the field by the beach as fast as their legs could take them. There, the albatross was waiting for them, sitting on the grass cawing and cawing and cawing with laughter.

"I think," the rabbit said, as he walked up to the albatross, wiping the egg of his fur, "we should really leave this to the professionals…."

THE END OF CHOCOLATE

"Ladies and gentlemen!" The voice coming out of the loudspeaker outside the town hall echoed down across the town square. "Please welcome your Lord Mayor, civic leader Fortescue!"

A pompous fanfare blared out of the speakers, as the equally pompous figure of Mayor Fortescue - dressed in his full regalia, with long fur robes, a golden chain and a ludicrous crown perched atop his head - strode out onto the balcony in front of the town hall.

"Good morning, everyone!" The Mayor exclaimed, awaiting a round of applause that never came. The crowd that had assembled outside the town hall to hear today's declarations looked on, unimpressed. Mayor Fortescue held these assemblies almost every day, and the people of the town had grown weary of his constant announcements, most of which had little purpose but to tell the people everything he had been up to. Today, however, was something different.

"As you will all no doubt be aware," Mayor Fortescue went on, "this weekend is Easter weekend. That means that all of us - every one of us - will be celebrating this by giving out our Easter gifts, by hunting Easter eggs, and by eating lots and lots of chocolate."

At the mention of chocolate, a few people in the crowd cheered, thinking ahead to the sweet treats they were all going to enjoy this weekend.

"But I, as your mayor," Mayor Fortescue continued, "cannot stand idly by while you indulge yourselves in such unhealthy practices. That is why, as of today, all chocolate is to be banned, across the entire town!"

"What!" Gasped the crowd.

"Boo!" Shouted some people at the back. "Boo!!!"

Mayor Fortescue tried to calm the unrest. "Now, now," he said, waving a finger in the air like a teacher telling off an unruly student, "it is for your own good. Chocolate is nothing but sugar and fat, you know. It's not good for you. Any of you. So as of today, its sale is forbidden in all the shops and cafes of the town!"

The crowd's murmurs of disapproval grew louder as the mayor pompously swept his way off the stage and disappeared back into the town hall.

A voice echoed out from the loudspeaker once more. "Just to confirm," it said, "that the sale of all chocolate, chocolate products, cocoa, and hot chocolate is henceforth forbidden in the town. All shops and cafes either stocking or selling chocolate products should be prepared to hand them over to the authorities at 10 o'clock this morning, or else be forcibly closed…."

The voice echoed on and on, as the new rules were officially read out and imposed on the town.

"Did you hear that?" Ivan said, turning to his best friend, George, who stood beside him in the crowd. They had been on their way to school when they had heard the mayor's fanfare and stopped outside the town hall to hear his latest announcement.

"Yes!" George replied. "And right before Easter weekend too! Mayor Fortescue has really gone too far this time."

At school, word of the mayor's latest rule change spread fast. The pupils watched from the classroom windows as police vans drove by, off into the town, to collect all the forbidden chocolates from the shops and stores.

"What do you think they'll do with it all?" Ivan asked George.

"They'll probably just destroy it, put it all in the bin," George answered disappointed, "just think - all that lovely chocolate, all going to waste."

Sure enough, the vans were soon on their way into town, stopping by every sweetshop, every corner store, every café, and every cake stop, collecting up all the chocolate treats that they had on sale, before taking them all back to the town hall. As they walked home from school that afternoon, Ivan and George looked in all the shop windows and saw empty shelves everywhere.

That night, Ivan lay in bed, tossing and turning, and thinking about what Easter was going to be like without chocolate. "It's unimaginable!" He muttered to himself. "No chocolate eggs at Easter? What a ridiculous idea."

He glanced over at the clock beside his bed. It was almost 3 o'clock in the morning. He hadn't had a wink of sleep yet. He turned over and pulled the cover up snuggly over his shoulders.

Just as he could feel himself drifting off to sleep, however, a noise outside woke him up. It was the sound of a car engine - or rather, a few car engines, running slowly and quietly in the street outside. Ivan leapt out of bed and ran over to his bedroom window and looked outside. All the police vans from the previous morning were slowly driving through the streets, under cover of darkness, heading straight for the town hall.

Ivan glanced back over at his clock to double-check the time. "That's odd," he thought to himself, "why are they all out like that in the middle of the night?"

He stood at his window and watched as the first van pulled up alongside the town hall, and its doors swung open. He watched too as Mayor Fortescue, still dressed in his ludicrous robes and his equally ludicrous crown, ran out of the front of the town hall, skipped gleefully over to the van and peered inside. Ivan saw him clap his hands with excitement, then scamper back inside the town hall. "What on earth is he doing now?" Ivan muttered to himself.

The town hall clock chimed the hour, and Ivan wearily walked back over to his bed and lay down. He would have to be up in a few hours for the last day of school before the Easter holidays, so had to get some sleep. But as his eyes closed, his thoughts were still focused on the vans trundling through town under cover of darkness, and Mayor Fortescue.

The following morning, Ivan and George were walking to school, when Ivan happened to mention the bizarre scene that he had seen the previous night. George stopped. "Wait," he said, "all the vans were going to the town hall? After dark?"

"Yeah," Ivan replied, "it was exactly 3 o'clock in the morning, because the town hall clock rang out while I was watching it all. Very strange."

George thought for a moment. He glanced down at his watch, then off towards the town hall. "Come on," he said, "we need to get to the bottom of this." And off he ran, down the main street of the town, towards the town hall.

"Hey, wait up!" Ivan shouted after him.

He caught up with George, who was standing at the tall gates outside the town hall peering through the metal bars, trying to see what might be happening inside. "What are you doing?" Ivan said. "We're going to be late for school?"

Just then, the gates swung open as one of the mayor's vans trundled out and off down the high street again.

"Come on!" George shouted, and he ran through the open gates and towards the town hall.

"George!" Ivan shouted as he ran in after his friend, the gates clanging shut just behind him. "What on earth are you doing?!"

The two boys stood on the grounds of the town hall and looked up at the imposing building in front of them. "There's something fishy going on here," George said, "and I think I know what it is. Come on."

Together, he and Ivan crept forward, up to one of the windows of the town hall, and peered inside. Everything looked perfectly normal. Then, they crept to the next window and peered inside. There, one of Mayor Fortescue's councilors was sat idly filling in some paperwork of some sort, while another sat typing away at a computer screen.

"Come on!" George hissed, as he and Ivan crept forward to the next window.

"Wait," Ivan said, "do you smell that? It smells like...," he looked at George, who was staring wide-eyed at his friend.

"Chocolate!" George replied. "I can smell it too! Come on, it's coming from this way...."

The boys crept onwards, around the side of the building. The delicious smell of chocolate grew stronger as they walked. As they reached the first building, they peered inside, and there was Mayor Fortescue - sat on a grand chair, at the head of an equally grand table, surrounded by all manner of chocolate treats.

Cakes. Muffins. Cookies. Chocolate bars. Chocolate eggs. Chocolate bunny rabbits. They were all piled high, all over the table, and all over the floor. And in the middle of it all, sat Mayor Fortescue - with melted chocolate all over his face and hands.

"Mmm, delicious!" The mayor exclaimed, as he picked up another chocolate egg, tore off its foil wrapper, and stuffed it - almost whole - into his mouth.

Ivan and George could scarcely believe their eyes. "Why, that crooked, lying, greedy old thing!" George hissed. "He's taken all our chocolate just to keep it for himself!"

At that moment, Mayor Fortescue happened to look up. His face dropped as he saw the two boys looking in at him devouring more than his fair share of Easter chocolate.

Ivan and George looked extremely angry and shook their heads as the mayor stood up and came running over to the window, and threw it open.

"Now, now, boys," he stammered, his teeth and lips stained brown with chocolate. "This - er, this isn't what it looks like!"

"Isn't what it looks like!" Repeated George. "Mayor Fortescue, you've taken everyone's chocolate in the entire town, and kept it all here for yourself!"

"Well," said the mayor, "that's not strictly true…."

"Uh-huh?" Ivan said, unconvinced. The mayor looked dejected.

"We, er… Well, we also bought in a lot of extra chocolate from the next town over too," he admitted, and he dropped his head with shame. "And the town next to that. And the town next to that!"

"You've taken all the chocolate from all the towns?" Ivan exclaimed.

"Oh, boys! I'm so sorry! You must forgive me, but it's just too delicious! I can't help myself!"

George again shook his head. "Mayor Fortescue," he said, "how could you!"

"I know, I know," the mayor went on, "it was foolish of me. I know it was wrong, but oh, chocolate is just too delicious! Now please, you have to promise me, you cannot tell anyone about this. My reputation! Think of my reputation! You must not tell anyone, please, I beg of you. I'll do anything you want."

The two boys looked inside at the huge mountain of chocolate - more than they had ever seen in their entire lives - and then at one another. "Okay," George said, "I have an idea."

Having made arrangements with the mayor, the two boys headed to school as usual and finished up all their work ahead of the Easter holidays. As the final school bell rang and all the pupils began filing out of the school gates, they heard a bizarre noise growing louder as they walked down the street. It was a mixture of shouting, laughing, car horns, and the silly pompous fanfare that the mayor's band always played.

Suddenly, ahead of them, a parade of vehicles turned into the street, all blaring their horns and blasting the mayor's music from their speakers. A crowd had gathered around the vehicles and were laughing and cheering as they followed them along the road. And there, stood on top of the first truck - dressed in a ludicrous rabbit costume, complete with long ears, but still wearing his crown - was Mayor Fortescue.

"Happy Easter!" He shouted. The kids watched as he delved into a large bag beside him, taking out huge handfuls of chocolates and cakes, and threw them into the crowd. "Happy Easter, everyone!"

RABBIT IN THE HEADLIGHTS

One evening in the middle of spring, a young farmer named Harry was cycling home from town along one of the long, winding lanes that led to his and his family's farmhouse. The sun was beginning to set, and it was becoming gloomy and a little misty under the trees, so Harry reached forward as he went and turned on the small headlamp tied to the front of his bicycle so that he could see the road ahead better.

It had been a long day. Easter weekend was approaching, and as the shops in town would all be closed for the next few days, Harry had had lots of errands to run. As he cycled slowly along, he found his mind beginning to drift and his thoughts turn to home, his family, the delicious meal no doubt waiting for him in the kitchen - and, of course, his bed.

Ahead, the lane curved gently around to the right, heading up along the side of the pasture in front of the farmhouse. But as Harry turned the corner on his bike, the glare from the setting sun shining across the open land suddenly caught him off guard, and for a moment he could scarcely see anything in front of him. He shielded his eyes as best he could with his hand, to make sure he didn't accidentally ride through one of the potholes in the bumpy road - or worse still, lose his way entirely and end up riding straight into the muddy ditch by the roadside. But it was too late. He felt the bike judder, and for a moment Harry was jerked up and down as if he had cycled over a fallen log or a large rock. He pulled the brakes, and the bike screeched to a halt.

With the glare of the sun still in his eyes, Harry fumbled in his pocket for his sunglasses and put them on. He looked down to check for any damage to the tires of his bicycle and, seeing nothing wrong, turned to look down the lane behind him to see what he had ridden over. Nothing.

"Strange," he muttered to himself. Harry was just about to continue on his way when he spotted something in the long grass by the roadside. Jumping off his bike, he wandered over and saw a tiny, pale rabbit crouched in the grass.

"Hello," Harry said. He bent down, expecting the rabbit to run away skittishly across the open field, but it just sat there in the grass. "Oh no," Harry went on, "I hope it wasn't you that I hit. Are you okay, little guy?"

Harry reached out and, to his surprise, the tiny little rabbit let him stroke his back. His fur was very soft, and his back felt damp from the dew coating the grass. "You look alright to me," Harry said, "here," and he plucked a few dandelion leaves out of the soil around him and held them in front of the rabbit.

For a moment, the rabbit seemed suspicious and appeared to stare up at Harry with a quizzical look on its face. But after a second or two, it sniffed the dandelion leaves and greedily gobbled them up.

"There you go," Harry said, "you're okay, aren't you, little guy."

Harry dropped a few more leaves in front of the rabbit, gave him one last pat, and began walking back to his bicycle when the rabbit slowly rose to its feet and hopped - or rather hobbled - after him. Harry turned to see the rabbit tottering out of the grass and into the middle of the road, limping slightly as it went.

"Oh, no!" Harry exclaimed, and he ran back over to the rabbit, picked him up, and bundled him carefully inside his jacket. "Let's get you home and take a look at what's wrong. We can't have you out here on your own all night if you're hurt."

Back at the farm, the injured rabbit soon became the talk of the house. Harry's mother, Annie, had wrapped a little woolen blanket around it, and now sat at the kitchen table cradling it in her arms to keep it warm. Harry's two children, Daisy and Cara, sat beside her looking concernedly at the rabbit as it snoozed in their grandmother's lap. Luckily, their mom Maria was a vet, and she too was due home any minute now from her practice in the city. She more than anyone would be able to tell what was wrong.

The back door swung open, and Harry walked in carrying a dusty old wire-framed rabbit hutch in his hands, filled with fresh hay. "I knew we still had this somewhere," he said, as he awkwardly walked his way into the room, only narrowly managing not to knock a pile of dishes off the dresser by the door.

"Careful, Harry!" Annie shouted. "Watch where you're going!"

Harry placed the hutch on the table. His arms and his shirt were covered in dust. "Phew!" he said. "It was right at the back of the garage, that thing. I had to pull almost everything out to get to it. How's the little guy doing?"

"He's sleeping, by the looks of it," Cara said, "mom will know best, though."

Just then, the sound of a car pulling up outside and the glare of headlights through the windows told them all that Maria was home from the city. "Right on cue," Harry said, "come on, kids. Let's go tell mom what's happened."

Once she had heard the story of the rabbit by the roadside, Maria carefully examined him for any signs of injury. "On the whole he's okay," she said to Harry, as she placed the rabbit inside the hutch, "but I think you might have run over the little guy's tail…"

Annie gasped. "Harry, you mean old thing!" She exclaimed. "How could you run your silly old bike over a little thing like this?!"

"It wasn't my fault!" Harry replied. "The sun was in my eyes; I could barely see anything! You're lucky I didn't cycle into the ditch and hurt myself."

"Pfft!" Annie shook her head. "Poppycock. You'd have been fine, I'm sure. Not like this poor little thing, eh?"

"Thank you, mom," Harry said sarcastically.

Annie bent down and peered through the wire of the hutch at the rabbit sitting peacefully in the warm hay inside. "Will he be okay, Maria?"

"Oh, yes, he'll be fine in a day or two," Maria replied. "There's nothing broken, I don't think. More than likely his tail is just a little bruised. A few days of rest and plenty of food and he'll be back up and hopping around, I'm sure."

"That's good news!" Harry said. "Come on, kids. Let's go and get out little some dandelions from the grass outside - the little guy seems to like those."

The following morning, Daisy and Cara were the first to come downstairs and check on their overnight visitor - and were amazed by what they found.

"Mom! Dad! Granny!" They shouted as they ran back upstairs to wake everyone up. The family gathered in the kitchen, all standing around the kitchen table looking down at the rabbit in the cage.

"Well, I'll be…," Harry muttered.

"Good gracious!" Annie said.

"I've never seen anything quite like it," Maria added.

Inside the cage, the rabbit was sat quite happily munching away on the pile of fresh dandelion leaves the kids had fetched him the previous evening. He looked perfectly fine and seemed to have much more energy than yesterday. The only thing was, he now seemed almost twice the size.

"He's so big!" Daisy said. "He wasn't that big yesterday, right, dad?"

"Absolutely not!" Harry replied. "I'd have known for sure if I'd cycled over something that big, he'd have thrown me over the handlebars!"

Inside the hutch, the rabbit hopped over to the bowl of water Harry had left him and took a drink.

"Oh, he's still moving a little awkwardly on that back foot," Maria said as she crouched down beside the hutch to take a closer look. "We'd better look after him another day or two. Kids, do you want to go and fetch some more dandelions from the lawn while dad and I fix breakfast?"

The following day was Easter Saturday, and Daisy and Cara were again the first ones awake. Just like the day before, they ran downstairs to check on the rabbit, and quickly scampered back upstairs shouting "Dad!", "Mom!", and "Granny!" once they saw him. And again, just like yesterday, the family stood around the kitchen table, scarcely able to believe their eyes.

The rabbit was sat inside the hutch, happily munching on the dandelions they had left for him - only this time, he was twice the size again. So large, in fact, that when he turned to take a drink from his water bowl, he almost knocked it over.

"Good gracious!" Annie exclaimed,

"I don't understand it," Maria muttered.

"I'd *definitely* know if I hit that thing," Harry said, "he's a monster!"

Daisy and Cara giggled as the enormous rabbit stared out through the bars of the hutch at them as he quietly took up another dandelion stalk and started eating.

"Come on," Cara said, "let's go get him some more from the grass outside," and off she and her sister went.

"He's still not walking as well as he should," Maria muttered, peering down through the bars of the hutch. "Better give him one more day before we set him loose, Harry."

The following day was Easter Sunday. Again, Daisy and Cara were the first ones awake, and again after they came down to the kitchen they ran back upstairs shouting "Dad! Mom!", and "Granny!"

And once more, the family assembled around the kitchen table, staring down at the hutch, unable to believe their eyes.

"What the…?" Maria said.

"Well, I never…," Harry muttered. "He's…. He's gone?"

"Ha, ha!" Annie laughed. "I knew it! Happy Easter, kids!"

Inside the cage - big enough to almost touch the sides - was a huge chocolate egg. And the giant rabbit was nowhere to be seen.

DAFFODILS

Every week, come rain or come shine, Seth did his paper round first thing in the morning, before most of the town was awake. He would get on his bike, cycle down to Mr. Hope's, who ran the local corner shop, pick up his bag of papers and deliver them to all the houses on his block. And each week, he would put a little of the money he earned from the paper round to one side, hoping one day to buy himself something he had always wanted: a brand new, top-of-the-range camera.

Seth's granddad had been a photographer for the local paper and had gifted him his first camera as a birthday present some years earlier. That had sparked Seth's longtime interest in photography - but his granddad's camera was understandably quite old, and was looking a little worse for wear. It was now better suited to being kept on the shelf in his bedroom and being admired as an ornament rather than taking pictures! So instead, Seth had set his sights on a brand-new camera that would take his pictures to the next level!

Week by week, he managed to put a little money aside. But then, out of nowhere, Seth's mom became sick.

It was a shock to Seth's family to find out how poorly she was, but her doctors were sure she was going to make a full recovery - she just had to take a few months of medication and rest up in bed as much as possible until she got better. That was easier said than done because Seth's mom had always been a very active, outgoing person. Before long, she had become fed up with being confined to her bedroom and was becoming very frustrated at not being able to get out and do all the things she always did.

After a few months, with spring fast approaching, Seth's mom was coming to the end of her medicine. Although she was feeling much better, the long course of treatment had taken its toll and she was feeling very tired, and more frustrated than ever. So, to cheer her up and celebrate the end of her treatment, Seth decided to surprise her.

His mom's favorite flowers were spring daffodils. Every spring, she would go out to the garden in front of the house, and tend to the daffodils that grew around their lawn - but this year, with her not being well, she hadn't had a chance to, and the flowers that were growing there were full of weeds and grasses, and in desperate need of someone with a green thumb. Seth had tried as best he could to keep the garden tidy while his mom had been unwell, but he wasn't much of a gardener. So instead, he came up with a plan to fill the lawn outside their house with as many bunches and vases of daffodils as he could.

Easter was fast approaching, and Seth decided that Easter morning would be the perfect day to put his surprise plan into action. So, a few days before, he told Mr. Hope all about it.

"Mr. Hope," he said. "I've come up with this brilliant idea. I'm going to surprise my mom on Easter morning with a garden full of her favorite flowers - daffodils."

"Oh, yes?" Mr. Hope said dubiously, as he sat behind the counter in his shop going through hall his paperwork. "And where are you going to get those from?"

"Well, I'm going to go round all the florists and flower shops in town, and all the gardening stores in the market place, and buy as many bunches of them as I can. Then I'm going to fill the garden with them so that when she looks out her window on Sunday, there'll be daffodils as far as the eye can see!"

"Ha!" Mr. Hope laughed. "You know these things cost money, don't you? Flowers are expensive, Seth! Where on earth are you going to find enough to buy that many?"

"Well," Seth replied, "I have my money from today's paper round, of course. But I was thinking could always do some extra jobs around town over the next day or two?"

"Hmm," Mr. Hope said ponderously, "I tell you what. The front window of my shop is filthy, and I can't get up there to clean it properly with my bad shoulder. Take the steps from the storeroom out back and clean the window for me, and I'll match the money from your paper round this week."

"Oh, wow, thank you, Mr. Hope!" Seth replied eagerly, and off he went into the storeroom and came back out with Mr. Hope's rickety old step ladder. He pitched the steps up at the front of the store while Mr. Hope fetched a sponge and filled a bucket with hot soapy water. Before long, the front window was gleaming in the spring sunshine - all except the very top corner.

"I can't quite reach this last little bit," Seth muttered to Mr. Hope, as he stretched up to the very top of the window.

"Oh, now, Seth," said Mr. Hope, who was standing holding the ladder steady, "you be careful, I wouldn't want…."

But it was too late. As Seth stretched farther than ever and finally wiped clean the very top of the window, he kicked back with his foot and knocked the ladder out of Mr. Hope's hands. "Waaah!" Seth shouted as he crashed down from the latter, landing on top of a display of fruit outside Mr. Hope's shop. "Waaah!" Mr. Hope shouted, as the bucket of now freezing-cold soapy water overturned and landed on his head.

"Uh, oh," Seth laughed, as Mr. Hope coughed and spluttered, and took the bucket off his head.

"Bah! Look at me!" Mr. Hope exclaimed. "I'm soaking wet!"

Seth couldn't help but laugh. "Well, at least your window is clean?!" He said.

"Ohhh…," Mr. Hope replied angrily, as he wiped the suds from his eyes. "Here," and he reached into his pocket, and took out the money he had promised Seth. "Right, take that and go and get your silly flowers while I go and get cleaned up!"

As Seth walked home, still laughing about Mr. Hope and the bucket of water, he walked past his neighbor's house. She sat on her front porch in the sunshine reading her book.

"Morning, Mrs. Anderson!" Seth shouted.

"Oh, morning Seth!" She called back.

"Say," Seth said, "I don't suppose you have any odd jobs that need doing around here, do you?"

Mrs. Anderson put down her book. "Odd jobs?" she said. "Well, yes, I do - oh, my, I always do. But whatever for?" She asked. Seth told her his plan to fill the garden with flowers. "Oh, Seth," she said, "that's so lovely. Your mom will love it!"

"That's what I'm hoping for," Seth said, "so, can I help you with anything?"

"I tell you what," Mrs. Anderson said, as she stood and walked down from her porch and along to her garden gate. "The storm drain, outside here." She pointed at the side of the curb. "It's all choked up with mud and leaves, I don't suppose if I were to get you some of my old gardening gloves you might be able to reach in and …."

"Say no more!" Seth said eagerly. "Consider it done."

Off went Mrs. Anderson to fetch some gloves, and within a matter of moments Seth was waist-deep in the drain, scrabbling around in the muck and the damp to clear it of leaves. "Oh, my," Mrs. Anderson said, as she looked down at Seth's legs kicking around above the ground. "Now, you be careful in there, Seth, I don't want you getting hurt."

"No problem at all," Seth said, throwing out another handful of leaves behind him, "it's almost clear, really. Aha!"

At that moment, he grabbed hold of one last big handful of wet leaves and with one final tug, wrenched them out of the drain and threw them up onto the road behind him.

Unfortunately, he didn't know that Mrs. Anderson was now standing right behind him, peering into the drain as he worked away - and the bundle of leaves and mud landed right in her face.

"Blurgh!" She exclaimed, as she toppled backwards and landed with a bump behind her. Seth scrabbled out of the storm drain, to find Mrs. Anderson sitting on the road, with mud and wet leaves and grass dripping off her face.

"Oh, no!" He said. "Mrs. Anderson, I'm so sorry."

"Oh," Mrs. Anderson said as she tried to laugh about it, "it's..., it's quite alright, I shouldn't have been standing there... Oh, dear me." As she wiped the mud from her face, she reached into the pocket of her cardigan and handed Seth the money she had promised him. "There you go, son. Now I really should go and get myself cleaned up..." And off she went back into the house.

"I'm starting to think these odd jobs might not be for me," Seth said a little disappointedly.

When he arrived home, Seth emptied his pockets onto his desk in the bedroom.

His two odd jobs had not gone quite as well as he had expected - and had earned him nowhere near enough to fill his garden with daffodils.

As he looked around his room, wondering what best to do next, his eyes fell on the large jar of money he had been saving up for the past few months. "Ah well," he said to himself. "I guess there's only one thing I can do." And with that, he unscrewed the lid.

The following day, Seth finished his paper round, and then rode his bike all around town, buying up as many bunches and pots of daffodils as he could find.

Once his backpack was full, he'd cycle home, hide them all in the garden shed, and then head back out again to another set of stores and market stalls. Before long, the shed was full, and he realized he had more than enough flowers to see the plan into action.

A few days later, on Easter morning, Seth awoke extra early and crept down from his bedroom, and out into the garden. There, he took all of the daffodils he had collected and covered the front lawn with them.

As the sun began to climb higher and higher, and the day began to warm, the garden was flushed yellow with hundreds and hundreds of bright spring daffodils. Seth stood in the middle of the garden and looked up at his mother's bedroom window and waited.

Before long, she was there. Seth watched as she gently pulled aside the curtains. And when she saw the garden full of flowers, she gasped and threw open the window.

"Seth!" She said. "Oh, Seth, what is this? It looks wonderful!"

"Happy Easter, mom!" Seth shouted up. His mom was beaming with joy. She hadn't looked so well and so happy in weeks, Seth thought.

"Two minutes," she said, "let me get sorted, and I'll come downstairs."

A moment or two later, Seth's mom appeared at the front door and stepped outside. The daffodils rustled in the light breeze, and they seemed to glow yellow in the morning sunshine. "Oh, Seth," she said with tears in her eyes, "it's so beautiful. What a lovely surprise! How on earth did you …."

"Oh, he did a few odd jobs," said a voice. Standing at the garden gate was Mr. Hope. Beside him was Mrs. Anderson. And behind them were a few more familiar faces - those of the florists and gardeners and stallholders that Seth had gone to so he could track down all the flowers he needed.

"Mr. Hope!" Seth said. "What are you doing here?"

He and Mrs. Anderson laughed. "Ha, ha!" She exclaimed, "well, your odd jobs didn't quite go to plan, did they, Seth?"

Seth looked sheepishly down at his feet and then smiled. "No, I guess not," he said.

"But we were all so touched by what you were planning for your mom," Mrs. Anderson continued, "that we thought you deserved a little surprise of your own. So, we all clubbed together and got you a little something."

"Happy Easter!" Mr. Hope said, and handed Seth a small parcel wrapped up with a yellow ribbon, the same color as the daffodils.

And as Seth unwrapped it, he held in his hands a beautiful brand-new camera.

AN EASTER GIFT

From almost the moment they were born, Xena and Xavier were constantly bickering.

As a twin brother and sister, you might have expected them to be the best of friends. But instead, there was something in their natures - something in their personalities - that caused them constantly to clash.

Even as babies, when they were placed beside one another in their cot, it wouldn't take long for one would kick the other, or for one to reach out and poke the other's arm, or pinch their cheek - as if purely trying to annoy them. Soon, their parents would have to step in to stop them and put them in separate beds.

As they grew older, their bickering only grew worse. It seemed as if nothing made the terrible twins happier than annoying, badgering, and pestering one another.

At school, they were originally sitting side by side in their classroom before their constant fighting again proved too disruptive. One day, for instance, Xena threw bright green paint in Xavier's hair. But when the twins' teacher confronted her about it, the paint, Xena explained, was to get back at Xavier, because he had placed an upturned drawing pin on her chair.

Yet the drawing pin, Xavier explained, was put on Xena's chair because she had scribbled all over his exercise book. But the scribbling, Xena explained in turn, was because Xavier had dipped the tip of her ponytail in a pot of glue!

On and on and on it went, until their teacher decided there was nothing more she could do, and with rolling eyes and a long, deep sigh, she had them sit at opposite ends of the classroom from then on.

At home, of course, sitting apart from one another wasn't possible. As a result, Xena and Xavier's parents were forever finding them brawling and shouting, kicking and punching, and teasing and tormenting one another. There was no end to the things they would do to annoy each other - but worst of all were the pranks.

The pranks, it had to be said, began with Xavier. For their fifth birthday, their granddad had bought Xena a new coloring book, and (somewhat unwisely) had bought Xavier a water pistol. Before long, he was using it to torment his sister like never before - squirting jets of freezing cold water across the living room at her when she was least expecting it, or jumping out from behind his bedroom door to soak her as she walked back from the bathroom.

Xena, of course, was quick to get her own back. One day, Xavier couldn't find his water pistol, no matter where he looked for it. That evening, his mother found it in the freezer, where Xena had placed it earlier that day in a bowl of water that had now frozen completely solid. It took more than an hour for it to thaw out.

To get his own back, Xavier bought a fake spider, with long hairy legs and a big rubbery body, and dangled it in front of Xena's face using their father's fishing rod as she sat reading her book one afternoon. The neighbors said they could hear the screams from their house two doors down. Xena, in return, crept into Xavier's room and stole all his tin soldiers, took them back to her room, and painted them all so that they looked to be wearing bright pink dresses.

Then one day, while Xavier was sitting in the garden one day having a glass of juice in the early morning sunshine, he was suddenly dowsed in ice-cold water, which was thrown out of the upstairs window all over him by Xena. To get his own back, as Xena was sitting enjoying the summer sunshine later that day, Xavier threw a handful of worms into her lap that he had dug out of the flower bed at the top of the garden.

Day by day, week by week, month by month, the twins' pranks grew steadily worse. Eventually, their parents had had enough and demanded that the pair start to be nice to one another.

"But I don't want to be nice!" Xavier shouted.

"And neither do I!" Xena answered back.

"Well, you have to try!" Their mother demanded. "We've had quite enough of your nonsense in this house, and it has to stop! You are brother and sister; you should love each other. But you two go on at each other all day, like cat and mouse!"

Xavier and Xena glared at one another angrily.

"Your mother is right," their father joined in, "you two never stop with the pranks and the mean tricks. Enough is enough. Now behave, the pair of you. No more pranks in this house."

"Quite right," their mother continued, "it's Easter in a few days, and your granny and granddad, and your aunt and uncle, are all coming over for Easter lunch. So, I don't want any mischief from either of you. I mean it. No more pranks!"

Xena and Xavier folded their arms and slunk off to opposite ends of the house.

Later that day, Xavier went to see his father, who was busy tinkering in the shed in their garden.

"Dad," he said, "I've been thinking about what you said about all our pranks."

"Yes…?" His father said dubiously, worried that he must have spent the afternoon working on some new and even more unpleasant scheme to play on his sister.

"I…, well, I think you're right," Xavier said quietly, "as much as Xena annoys me, she is my sister. And…, well, I'd like to do something nice for her."

Xavier's father could scarcely believe his ears. "You?" He said. "Do something nice for your sister?"

"Mm-hm," Xavier nodded, "I…, I feel bad, we do fight all the time. And I really do love her, you know."

"Oh, come here," his father said, and gave Xavier the biggest hug he could, "what did you have in mind?"

"Well, that's the thing," Xavier said. "I've really no idea. I have a great idea for a joke to play on her, but…."

"Stop right there," his father said, "remember - no more jokes. Look, why don't you…, I don't know, why don't make her something?"

"Make something?" Xavier repeated. "What do you mean?"

"Well, when you make someone something, rather than just buy them a present from the shop, it shows that you've put in a lot of time and a lot of effort into what you've done for them. It makes the gift a lot more meaningful, you know?"

"Oh, yeah, I see what you mean," Xavier considered.

And you know, Easter is coming up in a couple of days, and we'll be having all the family round for Easter lunch, of course. Why don't you make Xena something and give her it as a present?"

"That's a great idea!" Xavier announced. "But…, what could I make her?"

"Well," his father said, "what does she like? She likes reading and drawing, and she's learning to sew at school, your mom is helping her with that."

"Her dress," Xavier said, "her favorite dress - the burgundy-colored one that she likes to wear when we visit granny and granddad?"

"Oh, yes, the one your granny made for her, of course. She loves that. But I've seen the sewing you brought home from school that time, Xavier, it was a little messy, wasn't it? And I'm not sure you can learn to make a dress in three days…."

"No, no!" Xavier said. "I'll make her something to go with it! I know! Remember the little pendant that Xena got for Christmas that time, but that she lost on our school trip? I can make her another one of those."

"A pendant?" His father said. "How will you make a pendant? You'd need metal, for starters, and I'm not taking you down the hardware store to start buying things like that, that's the last place a kid should be…."

Xavier thought for a moment. "Metal," he muttered to himself. He looked around his father's workshop. There were all sorts of tools and machines and pieces of equipment that Xavier had no idea how to use. Suddenly, an idea came to him. "Wait there!" He said to his father and dashed back into the house.

A moment later he returned to his father's workshop holding half a dozen of his toy soldiers in his hand. "These are made of metal, right?" He asked.

"Oh, Xavier," his father said, "your soldiers? Really?"

"Well, you said I'd need metal, and these are made of metal, aren't they?"

His father picked one up and looked at it closely. "Well, yes, they're usually made of tin or something like that…."

"Yes!" Xavier exclaimed excitedly. "Okay, dad, I'm going to need your help..."

For the next few hours, the house was filled with loud banging and crashing noises. When Xena and Xavier's mother arrived home from work, she stared worryingly in the direction of the noise. Xena was sitting in the window drawing something in her notebook when her mother walked in.

"What on earth is going on out there?" Her mother said, staring worryingly out the window in the direction of the garden shed.

"Dad's making something, I think. I saw Xavier out there too, I've no idea what he's doing."

"Well, it better not be more mischief," her mother said, "remember what I said this morning?"

Xena closed her book and looked over at her mom. "Yeah, about that," she said. "I was thinking...," she sighed, as if reluctant to say what came next, "I was thinking you're right, you know, mom. I know Xavvy and I play tricks all the time, but I really do love him. He's my brother after all."

Her mother looked astonished. "What?" She said, open-mouthed.

147

"And ...., well, I'll like to get him something, for Easter. A present," Xena explained.

"Oh, Xena," her mother said, and just like their dad had given Xavier that morning, she gave Xena the biggest hug she could. "That's so sweet of you."

"I was thinking," Xena continued, as she tore a page from her notebook and showed it to her mom. "I was thinking of making him something like this?"

"Oh, Xena, is that - wait, are you suggesting...?"

"Yeah, it's no problem. I'd need your help, of course. But it's fine. I'm getting a bit too big for it now, anyway."

Her mother looked at the drawing, and then over to the corner of the room, where her sewing machine was sitting on a table. "Oh, Xena...," she said.

That weekend, the entire family came together at Xena and Xavier's house for a grand meal on Easter Sunday. Their father and mother were busy in the kitchen preparing all the food, and the twins sat at the table with their grandparents, their aunt, and their uncle.

"You two are unusually quiet," said their granddad suspiciously. "You've usually pulled one another's hair by now, or drawn on your face or some such thing…."

"Ha! ha!" Their grandmother laughed. "Your granddad is right, you two, you are being unusually well-behaved today."

"Well, it's Easter, isn't it?" Xena said.

"Yes, Easter," Xavier chimed in, "it's a special day for us all, isn't it?"

"Aww, you two are so cute," their aunty said, "aren't they?"

"Hmm…," their uncle muttered. He sounded unconvinced. "That usually means they're plotting something. There's probably be a toad on the table in five minutes, or something, knowing them."

"Oh, now, shush," their aunty scolded, as their grandparents laughed.

At that moment, Xena and Xavier's parents burst out of the kitchen, their arms full of bowls and platters of the most delicious-looking food you could imagine. "Sorry for the delay!" Their father said. "There were more vegetables to prepare than we had anticipated, but we've got everything ready now!" Together, they started placing the dishes on the table until there was nothing else to be seen.

"Goodness me!" Granddad exclaimed. "There's enough here to feed an army!"

Before long, they were all sitting down and enjoying the food. "So," dad said, "what were we all talking about?"

"We were just saying that those two," Xavier and Xena's uncle said, pointing suspiciously at them from across the table, "are being unusually quiet."

"Ha!" Their mother laughed. "Yes, they've been like this for a couple of days now, it's been bliss."

"They're up to something…," their uncle said, "mark my words."

"Oh, don't be so suspicious," their aunt said.

"No, no," their mother said, "I think Xena especially has been planning an Easter surprise…"

"See!" Their uncle replied, "I knew it!"

"A surprise?" Their granddad asked. "What kind of a surprise?"

Suddenly all eyes were on Xena. Now was the time to reveal everything. She reached under the table and pulled out a small parcel, wrapped in glittering green paper. She looked over at her brother sitting next to her.

"Happy Easter, Xavier," she said as she handed him his gift, "I made this for you."

"Oh!" Their grandmother exclaimed, holding her hands to her mouth. "Oh, how sweet!" Their parents looked on proudly, as Xavier reached below the table too.

"Wait," he said, "that's a coincidence. Because - well, Happy Easter, Xena," he said as he brought a small parcel out from under the tabletop, wrapped in glittering blue paper, and handed it to his sister.

"Oh, Xavvy!" She smiled. "You shouldn't have!"

"Well, neither should you," replied Xavier, looking down at the gift from his sister in his lap.

"Well, go on then, you two, open them!" Urged their father. He turned to Xena and Xavier's mother. "Did you know about that?" He pointed at Xena's present.

"Yes, I did, but - did you know about that?" She pointed at Xavier's present in reply.

"Yes, but…."

At that moment, the twins started tearing open their gifts, scraps of wrapping paper falling to the floor beneath their feet.

Xena looked down at the beautiful metal pendant in her hands. "Oh, Xavier, it's beautiful," she said. "It's just like the one granny got me that I lost last year!"

"I know," Xavier replied, "that's what I was hoping for. Dad helped me make it, and then I painted it so that it would match your…."

At that moment, he tore open the parcel in his lap and found himself holding a small fabric bag, made from the most beautiful burgundy fabric. It had a small buckle on the front, and inside were lots of little pockets, each one just large enough to a toy soldier.

"…your dress." Xavier finished, "wait," he said, "what - what's this?"

"I made you a bag for all your stupid toy soldiers," Xena said, "they're always lying all over the place in your bedroom, it's so annoying. At least this way, you'll have somewhere to keep them all in the same – wait," she paused. "Hold on a second. What did you make this out of?" She held up the pendant.

"My… My soldiers," Xavier said. He looked back down at the bag in his hands, "and this? What did you make this out of?"

"It's… It's the fabric from my burgundy dress," Xena said, "the one that matches…"

"Your pendant," Xavier added. The two looked at one another and smiled. "Oh, no, we haven't…," Xavier said.

"Oh, yes, we have," Xena replied, and laughed as she hugged her brother.

"See," their uncle said. "I told you they were up to something!"

THE 100TH DAY

Jamie ran downstairs as fast as his legs could carry him. It was Christmas morning, and he wanted to see whether Santa had brought him the video game he had been asking for months.

His parents were already up. Dad was in the kitchen making a start on breakfast, and mom was sipping a cup of coffee and putting Christmas songs on the radio. "Happy Christmas, Jamie!" She said as he ran into the room.

"Happy Christmas, mom! Happy Christmas, dad!" Jamie ran over to the tree and stared at the huge pile of presents beneath it. One, lying on top of all the others, looked decidedly family. Jamie gasped and grabbed it, and immediately started tearing off the wrapping paper. His dad came through from the kitchen, holding a cup of coffee and a box of chocolates.

"Looks like Santa got your letter alright," he said, his mouth already full of sweets. "Happy Christmas, Jamie." Jamie turned round and smiled, and ran over to the television to play his game immediately.

"Oh, really," Jamie's mom said, looking at his dad. "Are you already eating chocolates? It's barely even 7 o'clock in the morning!"

"Hey, if you can't have chocolate for breakfast on Christmas Day, when can you?" Dad said, picking out another candy from the box and throwing it into his mouth.

"Honestly, you two," mom said. "Jamie with his games and you with your sweet tooth. You'd not be able to last five minutes without either one!" She laughed. "You're both as bad as the other! And both as stubborn as mules!"

"Hey, that's not fair," Jamie said, as his game loaded up on the television screen. "I'm nowhere near as bad as dad with his sweets."

"No, no, no, no, no, I'm not having that," Jamie's dad laughed, "he's on that computer game whatchamacallit all day, every day! I'm nowhere near as bad as that."

"Dad," Jamie said, "you're literally eating a box of chocolates for breakfast. You have a bar of chocolate in your mouth right now."

"Well," dad said defensively, "for that matter, you're literally sitting in front of a video game right now."

"See what I mean!" Mom laughed. "You're both as bad as the other."

"Fine!" Dad said. "I'll not eat another chocolate for as long as he doesn't play a video game, how about that?" And he put the box of chocolates down on the table.

Jamie turned and looked at his brand-new game - that he'd been waiting weeks and weeks to play - loading up on the screen. He was torn between playing it and enjoying his day, or - more importantly - getting one up on his dad. "Fine!" He said, putting down the controller. "I'll stop playing for as long as he can stand not eating chocolates. I give it 10 minutes before he's got another one in his mouth and I win!"

"Ha!" Dad laughed, "10 minutes? Easy. How about 10 hours?"

Jamie looked a little unsure, but then his determination to win won through. "Let's try 10 days, more like," he said.

Now it was Jamie's dad's turn to look a little unsure. He glanced down at the open box of chocolates on the table. But again, he was determined to win. "10 days? Easy. How about 100?"

"A HUNDRED DAYS!" Jamie gasped.

Now it was mom's turn to look unsure. "You two...," she said, shaking her head. "Honestly, as bad as each other. No way will you manage 100 days. I'll be surprised if you can last 100 seconds. Now, who's for breakfast?"

"100 days," Jamie's dad repeated.

Jamie stood up, walked over to his dad, and shook his hand. "Fine. 100 days," he said - knowing full well that neither of them was likely to last that long....

Not playing his game on Christmas Day proved a lot harder than Jamie had anticipated, but he soon found that he forgot about it so long as he kept himself busy with other things. He zoomed into a new book his best friend had bought him and read all morning.

At lunchtime, his grandmom and granddad came round, and they had bought him a new pair of rollerblades that he was soon whizzing around the driveway on. Before he knew it, it was bedtime, and he'd not felt the need to play his game once.

Dad, on the other hand, was having a tougher time of it. All Christmas Day, everyone around him was opening and delving into boxes of candies and chocolates - and all day he wanted to join them. But somehow, he managed to hold back, and before long the day was finished.

The following day, the same thing: Jamie kept himself busy playing outside, and his dad kept his mind off his favorite sweet treats.

One day soon turned into two, then three, then four, then a week. After the new year, one week became two, then three, then four. And as the months went by, and Easter weekend rolled around, the 100-day deadline was fast approaching.

On Easter morning, Jamie again ran downstairs to find his mom pouring out cups of coffee, and his dad making pancakes for breakfast.

"Happy Easter, son!" He called out from the kitchen.

"Happy Easter dad, mom," Jamie shouted back. His eyes fell upon a huge chocolate egg in the middle of the table in the living room. "Oh, wow!" He shouted. He began tearing off its sparkling foil wrapper as his mom and dad walked in from the kitchen.

"Dad," Jamie said teasingly, "are you sure you don't want any chocolate?"

"Oh, that's a good point," mom said, glancing over at the calendar on the wall in the corner of the room. "Ha!" She laughed. "100 days is today! I can't believe it - you both managed it!"

"What!" Dad said. "You mean, today I can actually have chocolate? This stupid forfeit is over?!"

"Wait, you mean I can play my game?!" Jamie echoed.

Mom laughed. "Well, I never. Not in a million years would I have thought you two would have managed it. Yep, 100 days ends today. Well done, both of you!"

"Ha, ha!" Jamie laughed, "here," he said to his dad, handing him a piece of his Easter egg, "you've earned this, dad."

"Ha!" Dad chuckled, "100 days, who'd have thought it? Thanks, Jamie." He leant over and shook Jamie's hand, marking the official end of the bet. "I guess you can go and play your game now."

Jamie turned and looked at the box of his game, still sitting on his video console by the television. "Actually," he said, "it's such a nice morning. I think I might go rollerblading for a while if that's okay?"

"Wh…., really?" Mom asked, sounding surprised. "Sure, go right ahead. Your breakfast will be ready soon though, so don't go far."

Dad looked down at the piece of chocolate in his hands too. "You know," he said as he warmed his hands on his coffee mug, "I'm okay for candies right now. It's not even 8 o'clock yet, after all. I think I'll just have some fruit." And he rose and walked into the kitchen.

Mom sat down in the living room and laughed as she took a sip of her coffee. "100 days," she said. "It's an Easter miracle!"

CONCLUSION

And with that, we've come to the end of our collection of Easter stories.

From magical missing rabbits to unlikely wagers, and from forbidden chocolate to a flowery Easter surprise, we've certainly been through a lot in these last few pages!

Here's hoping that your Easter doesn't turn out to be quite so eventful for you as it was for many of the people in these stories, of course! But let's hope as well that it turns out just as well as it did for Jamie and his dad, for the Great Splendido and his magic show, and for the farmer whose injured rabbit was something of a celebrity bunny in disguise!

But no matter how you celebrate it - and no matter what you get up to - all that remains to say here is have a very Happy Easter!

Printed in Great Britain
by Amazon

20907965R00098